"Who'd marry an ornery cuss like you anyway?"

"I was sort of hoping

Mouth gaping, Melo___ full five seconds. She marrying this man for remember, had imagi___ at least a thousand tim____ imaginings had he ever used the words *sort of.*

He flashed her his lazy, sexy grin one more time. Just when her knees were starting to melt along with her resolve, he said, "By the way, do you have any cream and sugar?"

She thought about hitting him over the head with one of the trays, but she didn't see much sense in denting a perfectly usable item.

"What do you say, Mel?"

Since Melody didn't have much except her diner and her pride, she untied her apron and slapped it on the counter before stalking toward the door. "I say get your own darned cream and sugar."

Dear Reader,

What a special lineup of love stories Silhouette Romance has for you this month. Bestselling author Sandra Steffen continues her BACHELOR GULCH miniseries with *Clayton's Made-Over Mrs.* And in *The Lawman's Legacy*, favorite author Phyllis Halldorson introduces a special promotion called MEN! Who says good men are hard to find?! Plus, we've got Julianna Morris's *Daddy Woke up Married*—our BUNDLES OF JOY selection—*Love, Marriage and Family 101* by Anne Peters, *The Scandalous Return of Jake Walker* by Myrna Mackenzie and *The Cowboy Who Broke the Mold* by Cathleen Galitz, who makes her Silhouette debut as one of our WOMEN TO WATCH.

I hope you enjoy all six of these wonderful novels. In fact, I'd love to get your thoughts on Silhouette Romance. If you'd like to share your comments about the Silhouette Romance line, please send a letter directly to my attention: Melissa Senate, Senior Editor, Silhouette Books, 300 E. 42nd St., 6th Floor, New York, NY 10017. I welcome all of your comments, and here are a few particulars I'd like to have your feedback on:

1) Why do you enjoy Silhouette Romance?
2) What types of stories would you like to see more of? Less of?
3) Do you have favorite authors?

Your thoughts about Romance are very important to me. After all, these books are for you! Again, I hope you enjoy our six novels this month—and that you'll write me with your thoughts.

Regards,

Melissa Senate
Senior Editor
Silhouette Books

Please address questions and book requests to:
Silhouette Reader Service
U.S.: 3010 Walden Ave., P.O. Box 1325, Buffalo, NY 14269
Canadian: P.O. Box 609, Fort Erie, Ont. L2A 5X3

CLAYTON'S MADE-OVER MRS.

Sandra Steffen

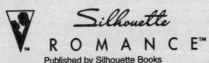

Silhouette
R O M A N C E™
Published by Silhouette Books
America's Publisher of Contemporary Romance

For Ann Green
After all these years, all our experiences, all our
wisdom, the only thing we know for sure is that we
still don't have a clue. Thanks, friend.

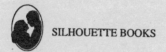 SILHOUETTE BOOKS

ISBN 0-373-19253-3

CLAYTON'S MADE-OVER MRS.

Copyright © 1997 by Sandra E. Steffen

This edition published by arrangement with Harlequin Books S.A.

® and TM are trademarks of Harlequin Books S.A., used under license.
Trademarks indicated with ® are registered in the United States Patent
and Trademark Office, the Canadian Trade Marks Office and in other
countries.

Printed in U.S.A.

Books by Sandra Steffen

SANDRA STEFFEN

Creating memorable characters is one of Sandra's favorite aspects of writing. She's always been a romantic, and is thrilled to be able to spend her days doing what she loves—bringing her characters to life on her computer screen.

Sandra grew up in Michigan, the fourth of ten children, all of whom have taken the old adage "Go forth and multiply" quite literally. Add to this her husband, who is her real-life hero, their four school-age sons who keep their lives in constant motion, their gigantic cat, Percy, and her wonderful friends, in-laws and neighbors, and what do you get? Chaos, of course, but also a wonderful sense of belonging she wouldn't trade for the world.

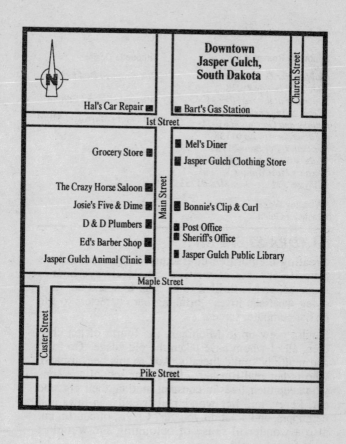

Chapter One

"Evenin', Mel."

For an instant everything inside Melody McCully went perfectly still. She recognized Clayton Carson's voice; more than anything, she recognized what it did to her, darn it all. In the second or two it took to recover her equilibrium, she pushed her hair out of her face and turned around. "The diner's closed, Clayt."

He ambled closer, sidestepping the tables she'd already cleaned off, coming to a stop on the other side of the counter where a handful of regulars would be ordering up breakfast in less than twelve hours. He surveyed the room the way he always did, leaning back on his heels, his fingers hooked through the belt loops of well-worn jeans. "Do you have any coffee left?"

Mel was tired, and when she was tired, she tended to be the tiniest bit cranky. Of course, Clayt claimed she was always cranky. That wasn't true at all. She had a perfectly fine disposition when it came to everybody else. It wasn't her fault that Clayton Ezekiel Carson was a blind fool who couldn't see the forest for the trees or the one woman in all the world who'd always loved him.

Motioning to the coffeepot with the wet dishrag in her hand, she said, "There's coffee, but it's been sitting in the pot so long it's about to turn into paint stripper."

"Just the way I like it."

Mel sputtered under her breath the entire time it took to reach beneath the counter for a clean cup and fill it with thick, black brew. For some reason Clayt hadn't moved. His eyes were in the shadow of the brim of his hat, and the lower half of his face was covered with a couple of days' worth of whisker stubble that did nothing to detract from the strong lines of his jaw and chin. The man was over six feet tall without the scuffed-up heels of his cowboy boots. He loomed over her, and Mel McCully hated to be loomed over.

Giving him a good once-over, she said, "You're too tall to talk to when you're standing. Unless you wanted that coffee to go, you might as well have a seat."

He lowered his frame onto one stool and dropped his hat onto another. "That hospitality of yours is something, Mel. Always keeps me coming back for more."

Mel McCully had been born and raised in a town chock-full of rugged cowboys, but Clayt Carson's slow, easy grin was one of a kind. She'd lost track of how many times she'd wished it wasn't. Sighing, she moved on to finish washing off the counter.

"Do you have to do that now?" he asked.

"If I want to get out of here anytime soon, I do. Why?"

She glanced over at him in time to see him flash her another lazy, sexy smile. "I was sort of hoping you'd join me."

"You were?"

This time his grin was accompanied by a brief nod. Reminding herself that she had plenty of backbone, she cast him a guarded look. His dark hair was a little on the shaggy side, and there were tiny lines beside his eyes and a crease slashing one lean cheek. He looked exhausted, whipped, dragged through a knothole backward. It served him right. Oh, she'd been as relieved as anybody when his little girl had been found safe and sound that very afternoon. No one knew why the little girl had run away, and Mel supposed Clayt had every reason to look worried and exhausted.

"Where's Haley?" she asked, taking a stab at conversation.

"She dropped off to sleep a little after six and hasn't moved since. Luke and Jillian are watching her at my place. With Haley asleep and Luke up to his elbows in wedding plans, I decided to go for a drive. I still can't believe my brother's getting married."

As owner of the town's only diner, Mel had heard all the jokes about the needy bachelors of Jasper Gulch. She hadn't said much when the local boys had decided to advertise for women to come to their small town, but when she'd learned it had been Clayt's idea, she'd nearly gone through the roof. He was her brother's best friend, and she'd been in love with him for as long as she could remember, long before Clayt had married someone else, someone beautiful and sophisticated and selfish, someone who had decided early on that Jasper Gulch wasn't for her and had left years ago. Recently Victoria had decided that motherhood wasn't for her, either. For three months now, Clayt had had custody of his nine-year-old daughter, and boy did he have his hands full.

It was true that there were sixty-two bachelors in Jasper Gulch and only six marriageable women, give or take a few who had moved in this past summer. Mel supposed she shouldn't have been surprised that Clayt had thought it was necessary to advertise for women to come to this godforsaken tract of land in South Dakota, but enough was enough. The town needed women, did it? What was she? Chopped liver?

"How about that cup of coffee?" he asked.

Swiping the back of her hand across her brow, Melody leaned her elbows on the counter. "If I drink coffee now, I'll never get to sleep."

He shrugged as if he thought he should have remembered that, then stared into the dark brew, lost in thought. Figuring it wouldn't hurt to be nice just this once, she said, "What's on your mind, Cowboy?"

His answer was a long time coming. "Haley, mostly."

"She's okay, isn't she?" Mel asked. "I mean, she didn't get into any real trouble last night when she was gone, did she?"

Clayt answered without looking up. "Not this time. But what about the next time? She's only been living with me for three months and she's already gone skinny-dipping with a boy, stolen food off people's front porches, and run away from home. I hate to think what she'll do next."

Mel's heart softened at the thought of Clayt's little girl, and so did her voice as she said, "Instead of trying to figure out what she's gonna do next, maybe you should try to figure out why she's doing the things she's doing."

"I think I know why."

"You do?"

"She needs a mother."

Melody went back to cleaning off the counter. Scrubbing at some dried-on ketchup, she said, "Most kids do, Clayt."

"Yeah, well, the first two single women to move out here passed me right over for my brother and my best friend. I guess there's no accounting for taste, huh?"

Mel rolled her eyes. "Who'd marry an ornery cuss like you, anyway?"

"I was sort of hoping you would."

Mel froze. Mouth gaping, she stared at Clayt for a full

five seconds. She'd been dreaming of marrying this man for as long as she could remember and had imagined his wedding proposal at least a thousand times. Not once in all her imaginings did he ever use the words *sort of.*

He flashed her his lazy, sexy grin one more time. Just when her knees were starting to melt along with her resolve, he said, "By the way, do you have any cream and sugar?"

She opened her mouth to speak but couldn't seem to make a sound. She thought about hitting him over the head with one of the trays, but she didn't see much sense in denting a perfectly usable item. Completely oblivious to her agitation, he said, "What do you say, Mel?"

Since Mel McCully didn't have much except her diner and her pride, she planted her hands on her hips and raised her chin at the haughty angle she'd perfected years ago. She untied her apron in a flash and slapped it on the counter before stalking toward the door. "I say get your own damn cream and sugar."

"Mel, wait!"

She didn't even break stride. "And lock up when you leave." The door slammed on the last word.

Clayt blinked. At the sound of her footsteps clomping up the stairs to the apartment overhead, he slowly rose to his feet. Tiredly dropping a dollar bill on the counter, he reached for his hat and headed for the front door where he turned the lock just as she'd instructed. *Demanded* was more like it. Scowling, he thought it was exactly what he should have expected from Wyatt's little sister. Mel McCully had always been as ornery as the day was long. Why had he assumed tonight would be an exception?

Other than a few vehicles that were parked in front of the Crazy Horse Saloon, Main Street was deserted. The town's only bar was normally booming on Friday nights, but most folks were exhausted after spending the better part of last night searching for Haley. Things would be back to normal as soon as everyone got a good night's sleep. Clayt needed eight hours' worth of shut-eye, himself, but when he woke up, he'd still have a huge problem.

The worst drought in twenty-two years was only a memory now, but the shortage of women in town was still as real as the moon in the sky. Clayt had hoped to find a mother for Haley in one of the gals who'd come to town this summer. Everything had seemed so logical last spring. The town council had voted on his idea to advertise for women, the local paper had printed some of the bachelors' comments, and bigger newspapers had picked up the story, nicknaming Jasper Gulch "Bachelor Gulch." Scores of women had come out to check out the Jasper Gents. Unfortunately, most of them had taken one look at the dusty roads, the meager stores and the limited job prospects and had kept right on going. Only a handful had stayed, and Wyatt and Luke had snagged the two prettiest ones. More women continued to trickle in from time to time. Clayt figured it was possible that he might find one to his liking...eventually.

Haley needed a mother now.

His little girl was as precocious as they came. Victoria had never been mother-of-the-year material, but her latest desertion had been hard on their little girl. Things might not have been so bad if Clayt's own mother hadn't gone out to Oregon to care for his ailing grandmother. Left on his own with his freckle-faced daughter, Clayt had reached his wit's end.

He'd always known Mel had had a crush on him, just as he knew *he* needed help with a capital *H*. Marrying Mel seemed like a perfect solution. She already loved him, she was good with kids, and he'd known her all his life. And best of all, she was nothing like Victoria. Mel was neither gorgeous nor sophisticated. Hell, she was as predictable as daybreak. Until tonight the only time she'd ever stunned him was when she'd kicked him in the shins when she'd been in the first grade.

I say get your own damn cream and sugar.

Hitching one boot onto his truck's running board, he rubbed the shin Mel had kicked all those years ago, but it was his ego that was smarting tonight. Cramming his hat on his head, he climbed into his muddy truck and started the engine. He'd planned to announce his and Mel's engagement at the barbecue he was throwing on Sunday in honor of his brother's recent betrothal. So much for things going according to plan.

Clayt rubbed his bleary eyes. He was exhausted. A man tended to get that way after spending eighteen hours searching high and low for a girl who'd gotten it into her head to run away from home. He still thought Haley needed a mother. What an understatement. But she was safe for now, sound asleep in a four-poster bed in the house her great-grandfather had built on Carson land. Clayt needed a good night's sleep, too. With a little luck he might just be able to come up with an alternative plan in the morning.

"Clayton, look at me!" Haley called.

Clayt's heart made it to his feet before he did. His first impulse was to run hell-bent toward Haley. His second was to beg her to climb down from the gate she was using as a balance beam. But he was afraid any sudden noises or movements might cause her to fall into the pen with the meanest bull in the state.

His brother, Luke, and Wyatt and Cletus McCully must have had the same idea, because all four men set off toward the corral at a clipped, though steady gait. Keeping his voice as level as possible, Clayt called, "That's good, Haley. How about hopping down from there and helping Isabell Pruitt with the decorations for Uncle Luke's engagement party?''

Clayt hoped old Isabell didn't see his darling daughter stick out her tongue. ''That's sissy stuff,'' Haley complained. ''I'd rather help you, Clayton.''

She started to climb down, teetered slightly, then hopped to the ground. Four men breathed a collective sigh of relief but Clayt was the only one who placed his fist over his rapidly beating heart. Turning to his brother, he said, ''As soon as this barbecue's over, I'm moving that bull to the other pen.''

Luke and Wyatt both nodded but Cletus McCully shook his craggy head and said, ''It won't make any difference, boy. If there's trouble to get into, that girl's gonna find it.''

Haley chose that moment to stoop down to pet a half-grown kitten. Her stance reminded Clayt of how she'd looked when she was four, all little girl grace and innocence. He didn't know how a child could go from precociousness to sweetness in the blink of an eye, but his daughter had been doing it all her life. She'd come into the world squawking her head off, and had learned to walk when she was only nine months old. He'd only seen her for a week at Christmas and during the summers after the divorce, but he distinctly remembered the year freckles had started spattering her nose. She'd been seven. That was about the same time she'd started calling him Clayton. Not Daddy, not even Clayt. *Clayton.* Until Haley, only his mother had gotten away with that.

At first he'd thought it was just a phase. After a month, he'd asked her to call him Dad. She'd raised her chin and refused. Cajoling hadn't worked either.

He was the first to admit that he'd never known how to handle his little girl. But that hadn't kept him from loving her. She'd spent the seven years since the divorce being bounced from one end of Texas to the other while Victoria searched for the oil tycoon of her dreams. Clayt had custody now, and Haley was here to stay.

While Cletus, Wyatt and Luke set off to see how the women of the Ladies' Aid Society were coming with the rest of the food, Clayt put his hat back on his head and strode toward the barrel roasters where a side of beef had been cooking all night. Keeping Haley in his line of vision, he breathed in the aroma wafting on the breeze.

It was the third day of September and fall was in the air. The weather could turn on a person this time of year, but for now the skies were sunny and the air was comfortably warm. Picnic tables had been set up on the grassy slope of land between his folks' place and his own. The fine citizens of Jasper Gulch would start arriving soon. It looked as if the barbecue he was throwing for his only brother, Luke, and their best friend, Wyatt McCully, and their future brides was going to come off without a hitch.

Clayt was in a much better frame of mind this afternoon. Sleep had helped, but so had the realization that the situation with Haley wasn't completely hopeless or out of control. Oh, Mel's response to his marriage proposal still rankled, but the truth was he'd always done better when he was on edge, when beef prices were lousy and the weather was worse and only backbreaking long hours and sheer determination put food on the table and a little money in the bank. Somewhere between Friday night and noon today he'd decided it was about time he applied that same kind of sheer determination to finding a mother for his child.

Mel had had her chance. From now on he was going to check out the other women who lived in Jasper Gulch.

He was tall, Mel had said so herself. Women liked tall men, didn't they? Folks had always claimed he and Luke had gotten their father's looks and their mother's brains. Who was he to argue? So what if Mel had turned down his proposal. There were other fish in the sea. Okay, there weren't many, at least not in this corner of South Dakota. But there were a few, and by God, it was high time they were exposed to a large dose of Clayt Carson's charm.

"Wonders never cease, do they, girl?" Cletus McCully surveyed the folks talking and laughing in small groups throughout Clayt's side yard.

Mel downed the last of the punch in her paper cup before agreeing with her grandfather. It *was* amazing that two of the local boys—one of them her very own brother—were going to be married in a double ceremony in less than a week. It just so happened that she was immensely happy for her brother, Wyatt, and for Luke Carson, too. Jillian Daniels's red hair and surprising flare of temper was a perfect match for that Carson obstinacy. And Lisa Markman's throaty laughter and bad-girl smile was exactly what Wyatt needed.

Some things had definitely changed in good old Jasper Gulch. Others, however, remained the same. Tomorrow was Labor Day, and the day after that school would start, just like it did every year. The same people who'd attended the town picnic earlier that summer had turned out for Clayt's barbecue today. Punch had been ladled and plates had been emptied. Isabell Pruitt, the self-appointed leader of the Ladies' Aid Society, had checked the punch for possible spiking every fifteen minutes like clockwork. Now, children were jumping puddles near the barn door, mothers were fussing about muddy shoes, and the area ranchers were lamenting over the price of beef, just like they always did.

A trill of laughter drew Mel's gaze to a rough-hewn fence near the shed. Clayt straddled the top board and Brandy Schafer, the only girl from her graduating class a few years back to stay in Jasper Gulch, was laughing up at him with stars in her eyes. It was enough to turn Mel's stomach.

She'd always considered herself a reasonable woman, but the despair and disappointment she was feeling came from a place beyond logic or reason, a place that ached with shimmery emotions and dusky yearnings and hidden dreams.

Cletus muttered something under his breath and shook his head. "Don't take it to heart, girl. I'm sure nothing will come of that. One of these days Clayt Carson's gonna wise up and figure out that he couldn't do any better than you. Nobody could. Maybe it would help if you were a little nicer to him. A person catches a lot more bees with honey, you know."

Mel released a huge sigh and shook her head. She'd been doing that a lot since Clayt had *sort of* asked her to marry him. She'd stood in front of her mirror for a long time Friday night. She was twenty-nine years old, and she admitted that she was a little on the scrawny side. But her legs were thin and muscular, and although she wasn't exactly well endowed in the chest department, she thought her breasts were, well, nice, maybe even pretty in a pert, cute sort of way.

Casting another glance at the cleavage visible above the low neckline of Brandy Schafer's shirt, Mel cringed. Puppies were cute. So were kittens and bunnies and newly hatched chicks. But as far as breasts were concerned, it seemed that men preferred them in larger, more lush sizes. Cute breasts evidently ranked right up there with marriage proposals that included the words *sort of*.

Smoothing her thumb over the strands of hair secured in a heavy braid over her shoulder, she glanced up at her grandfather. Something had been bothering her ever since she'd stormed out of her own diner Friday night. She'd been hiding her feelings from Clayt for years. Yet he'd acted as if she should fall at his feet at her first opportunity to marry him. It didn't make sense. Neither did the fact that her grandfather seemed to know about her crush, too.

"Would you tell me something, Granddad?"

Cletus raised his bushy white eyebrows. "I'll do my level best, girl."

Checking to make sure nobody was within hearing distance, she whispered, "What makes you think I have tender feelings for Clayt?"

Cletus shifted from one foot to the other the way he always did when he was discarding answers faster than he could come up with them. Inching closer, he said, "I've known for years."

"You have?"

The nod of his head was more serious than Mel would have liked. "Now might not be the time to break this to you, but everybody knows."

Her hand flew to her throat. "That's impossible. I've never told a soul."

"When has that ever had anything to do with anything in Jasper Gulch? Would you looky there? Doc Masey's motioning for me to join him behind the shed for a nice fat cigar."

"Granddad."

He turned around again on bowed legs, although he could have pretended he hadn't heard.

"Everybody knows?" she mouthed.

Pulling at his suspenders, he said, "If you don't believe me, ask around." Without another word he headed for a group of his buddies who were waiting near the shed.

Mel stared after him, shaken. If everybody knew about her foolish heart's stupid infatuation with that ignoramus Clayt Carson, she'd never be able to hold her head high in the diner again. How could they have possibly known? She and Clayt were rarely civil to each other, let alone nice.

Why, then, had her grandfather said that everybody in town knew about her feelings? Cletus McCully was a wonderful man. He'd taken her and Wyatt in after their parents had drowned in the Bad River when she was six, and she loved him to pieces. The man would lay down his life for her and Wyatt, but Mel happened to know that he wasn't above bending the truth every now and then. He had to be mistaken about this. Still, he'd told her to ask around. Spying Jillian Daniels, one of the brides to be, Mel knew exactly where to begin.

"A double wedding. Isn't that, like, the most romantic thing you've ever heard of? And look at Lisa's dress. Isn't it, like, the most gorgeous dress you've ever seen?"

Clayt was doing his best to follow Brandy Schafer's conversation. But it wasn't easy. At first he'd blamed it on the upper swells of her breasts she was so intent upon showing him. Now he realized there was more to his distraction than her young, nubile body. Truth was, she was boring him to death.

"I mean, I adore that color of blue, and I love the way the material practically skims her ankles. If Lisa's going to carry that style of dress in her shop I'm absolutely positive the Jasper Gulch Clothing Store is going to be a success. Oh, I hope she does. I'm so sick of Western skirts and blouses…"

Idly, Clayt wondered how much longer the girl could keep talking without coming up for air. A movement out of the corner of his eye caught his attention. He didn't have to turn his head to know it was Mel McCully. He would recognize her slender build and dark blond hair anywhere. She was one gal who'd never bored him with useless prattle. Mel wasn't like other women. That's what he liked about her. He was all set to flash her his famous grin, but she walked right on by without a backward glance, and he ended up shaking his head instead.

So, good old Mel was holding a grudge. He wasn't surprised. She was more ornery and obstinate than any woman he'd ever known—including Victoria. Only Mel wasn't nearly as mean. Clayt didn't like thinking about Victoria. It reminded him of too many mistakes, of too many things he couldn't change. He'd married young. And he'd married wrong. He was thirty-six years old now. The next time he got married he'd like to do it right. Maybe not for love, but at least for the good of Haley.

He nodded at whatever in Sam Hill Brandy was talking about now. Mentally he checked her off his list. She was built nicely, but criminy, any woman who was going to stay a step ahead of Haley had to have a little more between her ears.

A new woman named Brittany Matthews had moved to town a couple of weeks ago. She'd pretty much kept to herself since her arrival, but Clayt had heard that she and her five-year-old daughter had come all the way from New Jersey. Old Mertyl Gentry had her cornered over by the food table right now. As soon as he could get a word in edgewise with Brandy, he'd mosey on over and introduce himself. Brittany. Now that was a real pretty name.

Chapter Two

Brittany. Brittany. Brittany.

It was all Mel had heard all day at the diner.

She placed the half-full tray of dishes on a table and headed for the front, where the Anderson brothers were waiting, money in hand. She smiled at Lisa, Jillian and DoraLee Sullivan on her way by, nodded at Brittany Matthews and stuck her nose in the air as she passed Clayt.

"Everything all right, boys?" she asked when she reached the register.

Neil Anderson nodded, but Mel had her doubts that he'd actually heard her question. He was too busy talking about the same thing everybody else was talking about.

"Brittany," he repeated quietly to one of his brothers. "The name has a nice ring to it, don't it?"

"Sure does," Ned declared. "I don't think Clayt's taken his eyes off her since they sat down in that booth, do you?"

"Nope," Norbert agreed. "And I can see why."

Ned nodded. "She's easy on the eyes, that's for sure. I'm not usually partial to short hair, but I'm making an exception for her. What do you think, Mel?"

Mel thought she felt a headache coming on. A glance at Clayt and Brittany made her sure of it. There wasn't really anything wrong with Brittany Matthews. She wasn't much taller than Mel, but the boys were right. Her brown eyes were friendly, and Mel could see how a man might find her dark, wispy hair the tiniest bit enticing. Clayt must have thought so, too, because he reached across the table and brushed a strand off her cheek.

Mel's temples throbbed like a set of bongo drums.

"Clayt's a lucky dog."

"Always did have an eye for the lookers."

"Ain't that right, Mel?"

The three thirty-something ranchers stopped short all at once, only to cast furtive glances at Mel one at a time. The brothers were slight of build and pretty good guitar players, but they'd never mastered the fine art of talking with a size-ten boot in their mouths. As if on cue, they flung enough money to cover their lunches onto the counter and took turns mumbling under their breath.

"Keep the change, Mel."

"Yeah, keep the change."

"S'long."

"Thanks, boys." While Melody punched the sale button on her old-fashioned cash register and deposited the money inside, Neil, Ned and Norbert moseyed out the door.

So, the Anderson Brothers knew, too.

Her grandfather had been right. Two days ago she'd been appalled at the very idea that people might know about her pathetic feelings for Clayt. She'd broached the subject with Jillian Daniels first, hypothetically of course. Jillian had seen through her carefully schooled expression like a picture window. Nodding her head as if trying to soften the blow, Jillian had said that Luke might have mentioned something to that effect. Lisa Markman's reply had been a little more straightforward, and although Wyatt had tried to hem and haw his way out of it, he'd ended up admitting that he'd known for years, too.

When she'd first discovered the truth, she'd been certain she would never be able to hold her head up in public again. Her pride *was* smarting, but after a little soul-searching she'd come to the realization that nothing had really changed. She was just in on the secret, that was all. Some secret it had turned out to be.

"Afternoon, Mel."

Mel could blame the fact that she hadn't heard Clayt's approach on the whir of the fan in the corner and the noise she was making stacking dishes on a tray, but she blamed the rapid thud of her pulse on something else entirely. Stiffening, she wiped her hands on her short apron and moved toward the cash register once again. "Everything to your liking?" she asked stonily.

"Your food's always good and you know it."

She glanced across the room in time to see Brittany Matthews disappear inside the ladies' room. Lisa, Jillian and DoraLee appeared to be finishing up with the wedding plans they were making at a table near the window, which left Mel on her own with Clayt for the first time since he'd *sort of* asked her to marry him four days ago.

Bristling all over again, she said, "That'll be seven dollars and sixty-five cents."

He handed her a ten. "How long you gonna stay mad at me?"

She cast him her most withering glare. "I've always been mad at you, Clayt Carson."

He shook his head the same way he always did. Holding out his hand for his change, he said, "Don't I know it. Things would be a lot simpler if you weren't so confounded contrary."

Shifting her weight to one foot, Mel took a chance and looked him straight in the eye. "How romantic."

"*You* want romance?"

As if realizing he'd spoken louder than he'd intended, he glanced around to see if anyone had heard, leaving Mel a moment to hide her feelings. She swallowed and blinked and swallowed again. It wasn't the question that hurt, it was his emphasis on *you*—as if she was the last person on earth he'd think about in a romantic way.

Thankful for the pluck she'd inherited from her grandfather, Mel straightened her spine and punched the button that would open the cash register drawer. "You and Brittany looked pretty cozy a few minutes ago. What's the matter? Is there something wrong with her, too?"

Either Clayt failed to hear the sarcasm in her voice or he chose to ignore it. Depositing his change in his pocket, he said, "No, Brittany's great. But she's having her own problems with her little girl, and God knows I'm having trouble with mine. We decided it probably wouldn't be a good idea to put the two of them together. I'm tellin' you, Mel, you could have made this a lot easier."

Brittany joined Clayt before Mel could think of a proper response, and the two of them strode out the door. Mel stared after them, wondering why she couldn't just get over him once and for all. What was so great about Clayt Carson, anyway? His ego went right off the top of the size chart, and God knew his skull was thicker than most. He'd always riled her, and he probably always would.

"You've gotta face it, sugar."

Mel jumped for a second time in a matter of minutes, only to find Jillian, Lisa and DoraLee staring at her from the other side of the counter. "What did you say?" Mel asked.

DoraLee slanted her a soft smile. "I'm afraid that one of these days you're gonna have to face the fact that Clayt Carson's never gonna wake up where you're concerned."

DoraLee knew, too. That, at least, wasn't so surprising.

DoraLee Sullivan, the sole proprietor of the Crazy Horse Saloon, was pushing fifty. She'd had a hard life, and it showed, but she had a knack for keeping the local boys in check no matter how many beers they'd had. She was also the closest thing to a mother Mel had had in a long, long time.

Leaning closer, Jillian covered Mel's hand with her own. "If it's any consolation, I think that future brother-in-law of mine is blind."

"That's right," Lisa said with a wink that had probably gotten her into a lot of trouble in her day. "If you want, I'll have Wyatt arrest him."

Glancing out the window to where Clayt was crossing the street, Mel said, "I don't think that will be necessary, Lisa."

She watched Clayt as he waited for Roy Everts to chug on by in his rusty, rattletrap of a truck. With a small wave and a smaller nod, he continued to the other side of the street.

The local folks claimed the only crimes in Jasper Gulch were jaywalking and gossip. There *had* been that little episode involving a pie thief a few months ago, and Lisa's car *had* been missing temporarily. And then there was that horrible color of orange Bonnie Trumble had painted the Clip & Curl. As far as Mel was concerned, Clayt Carson's cowboy swagger was the biggest crime of all.

"Aw, sugar," DoraLee crooned. "I don't want to hurt your feelings, but I'm afraid it's time you faced the fact that he's never gonna pop the question you've been waiting all your life to hear."

Mel sighed. "What would you say if I told you he already has?"

"He already has what, sugar?"

DoraLee's question drew Mel's gaze from the window.

All three women had leaned closer, and all three seemed to see the light at the same time.

"Do you mean..."

"...my future brother-in-law..."

"...asked you to marry him?"

There wasn't much Mel could do except nod.

"How?"

"When?"

"Where?"

Tipping her head toward a spot a little farther down the counter, Mel said, "He *sort of* popped the question right over there on Friday night."

"I had no idea," Jillian whispered.

"What did you say?" Lisa asked.

Mel shifted uncomfortably. "What do you think I said? I have a little pride, after all. I mean, what would you have done if Wyatt or Luke had said they were *sort of* hoping you'd marry them?"

Eyeing Mel with knowing brown eyes, Lisa said, "One thing comes to mind, but it isn't very nice. What did you do?"

"I left him sitting with the worst cup of coffee he'd ever tasted while I stormed up to my place."

"How awful," Jillian murmured.

"Yes." Mel's lips twisting snidely. "You can see how disappointed he is."

"No," Jillian replied, "I meant for you. How awful for you."

Mel sighed all over again. "Is it so wrong to dream of a little romance?"

DoraLee patted her bleached blond hair with one hand. "Maybe Boomer should give Clayt a few lessons in the romance department."

The blossoming relationship between Boomer Brown and DoraLee Sullivan was another thing that had changed in Jasper Gulch, but DoraLee was right. There was nothing romantic about *sort of.*

Sighing, Mel whispered, "I want him to notice me. As a woman. As a desirable woman. Just look at me. Pretty silly, huh?"

"But you're beautiful," Jillian admonished.

"Yeah, right."

"You are," Lisa insisted. "I noticed the first time we met."

"Your beauty doesn't flash like a neon sign," Jillian said quietly. "It's more subtle than that. Yours is the kind of beauty a person notices a little at a time."

DoraLee nodded her head, a tender expression crossing her round face. "Shoot, sugar, I thought you knew that."

Mel took her time looking into these three women's eyes. Smoothing her fingers over the thick strands of hair secured in a loose braid over her shoulder, she said, "I appreciate the votes of confidence, but if I'm so danged beautiful, why hasn't Clayt ever noticed?"

The expression in Lisa's dark eyes changed. She drew Mel away from the cash register and circled around her. Within seconds DoraLee and Jillian were doing the same.

"Hmm," Jillian murmured.

Chin in hand, Lisa said, "Are you thinking what I'm thinking?"

Jillian nodded. "I think it's time she made him notice, don't you?"

Mel eyed them both skeptically. "What do you mean?"

"How long have you worn your hair in a braid?" Lisa asked.

Without waiting for Mel to answer Lisa's question, Jillian asked another. "Has Clayt ever seen you in a dress?"

Looking to DoraLee for help, Mel said, "He's seen me in that blue jumper I wear to church."

"Mel," Lisa said, "how would you like to open Clayt Carson's eyes once and for all?"

Fingering her hair with one hand, Mel thought about the way Clayt had smoothed Brittany Matthew's short wispy strands off her cheek. "What would I have to do?"

Lisa sidled up to her. "The question is what are you willing to do?"

Mel looked at Lisa, and then at Jillian, but it wasn't until she'd met DoraLee's smiling blue eyes that she said, "What do you have in mind?"

DoraLee rubbed her hands together and laughed out loud. "Ooo-eee. Clayt Carson isn't going to know what hit him."

"And I know the perfect time and place for the unveiling," Lisa stated.

"At our double wedding," she and Jillian said at the same time.

Mel tried to protest that that was only four days away, and Lisa and Jillian had too much to do already. Lisa and Jillian exchanged knowing grins.

"There's plenty of time."

"You just leave everything to us."

Swallowing the trepidation that was fast becoming a fist-sized knot around her vocal chords, Mel hoped to high heaven she didn't live to regret what she was about to do.

Organ music was playing softly when Mel slipped into a pew near the front of the church. Unobtrusively gliding to the center of the row, she glanced around to see if anybody had noticed.

So far, so good.

Candles flickered on the altar and on windowsills throughout the old-fashioned church. Daisies and mums tied up with white bows and pale yellow ribbons adorned the front of the church and the end of every pew. The church was a hundred years old, yet it was filled with a sense of excitement and urgency it hadn't seen in a long time.

Wedding guests had started arriving twenty minutes ago, but it seemed that half of them were making a fuss over Hugh and Rita Carson, Luke and Clayt's parents, who'd arrived home from Oregon yesterday morning. The other half—all area ranchers and cowboys—were tripping over each other in their efforts to draw Brittany Matthews into conversation. As a result, no one had paid any attention to the petite woman in the peach-colored dress who'd hugged the shadows in her efforts to remain unnoticed.

Mel smoothed her hand over the soft fabric of her dress and crossed her legs the way she'd practiced. She recognized most of the voices coming from the back of the church, from Boomer Brown's booming baritone to Isabell Pruitt's annoying whine, all the way to DoraLee's infectious laughter. Today's wedding would be the first in more than five years and the only double wedding in the history of Jasper Gulch. Automatically reaching for the braid that was no longer hanging over her shoulder, she smiled to herself. Melody McCully planned to make a little history of her own.

Talking in undertones, guests began filing in. A short time later Boomer ushered Clayt's parents to the front pew on the right, while Jason Tucker ushered Ivy Pennington, a special guest of both brides, to the seat next to Mel. She smiled at the gray-haired lady, then glanced up to gauge Jason's and Boomer's reactions to the new Melody McCully. Looking stiff and uncomfortable in their suits and ties, they nodded nervously then hurried to the back of the old church, none the wiser.

Mel settled herself more comfortably in her seat and smiled to herself. Things were working perfectly. At this rate Clayt was going to be the first person to notice her, exactly as she'd planned.

Louetta Graham began to play another song on the organ, and the grooms took their places at the front of the church. Clayt, best man to both Luke and Wyatt, fell into line a few feet behind them. All three men were tall, all three were wearing dark suits, all three were handsome in their own right. Mel loved her brother, and she liked Luke Carson, but her heart beat a steady rhythm for Clayt alone.

His hair looked freshly cut and appeared darker beneath the flickering light of so many candles. His face was clean-shaven, his skin stretched taut over high cheekbones and that angular chin that could be so infuriatingly condescending. His nose was a little too wide to be considered aristocratic, and today his gray eyes looked serious and thoughtful.

At the first strains of the wedding march, everyone rose to their feet. Feeling tall in her new heels and giddy with joy and excitement, Mel held perfectly still, waiting for the moment when Clayt's eyes would meet hers.

Clayt could see Luke and Wyatt in his peripheral vision. It had taken everything he could think of to keep them calm this past hour. The hard part was over. Now, all he had to do was hand them the rings at the appropriate time and his job would be done.

Patting his right pocket where he'd placed Luke's and Jillian's rings and his left pocket where he'd tucked Lisa's and Wyatt's, Clayt peered through the crowd where the first bridesmaid was slowly making her way to the front of the church. Jason Tucker almost fell out of his seat as Allison Delaney floated by. If Haley was half as graceful at sixteen as Allison, Clayt was going to be in big trouble. The woman who came next didn't look old enough to be Allison's mother, but he'd met Corinna Delaney, the maid of honor—a newlywed herself and a close friend to Jillian and Lisa from when they'd lived in Wisconsin—at the rehearsal last night, and she was definitely Allison's mother.

His vision blurred, and for a moment he saw only a patch of pale peach. Before his eyes could focus, an "Ahh" wound through the church, and he turned his head slightly as Cletus McCully came into view, a red-haired bride on one arm, a dark-haired bride on the other. Clayt's mother always said there was no such thing as a homely bride, but Lisa and Jillian were prettier than most. As Jillian took Luke's arm and Lisa took Wyatt's, Clayt felt a burgeoning sense of pride that he'd been instrumental in bringing these two women to Jasper Gulch.

Listening with only one ear to the words Reverend Jones was reciting from his frayed prayer book, Clayt patted his pockets one more time then glanced at the people who filled the old church. He'd never seen so many ranchers and cowboys without their hats, but he had to hand it to them—the local boys didn't clean up too badly. His parents were sitting with Haley in the first pew across the aisle, and Opal Graham was sniffling into a lace handkerchief. Cletus McCully looked about as proud as he could be, and Ivy Pennington, the gray-haired lady sitting next to Cletus, dabbed at a tear on her cheek. Clayt caught sight of that peach-colored dress again, but before he'd gotten a good look at the woman wearing it, Reverend Jones asked everyone to take their seat.

Clayt glanced away and back again so quickly his vision blurred. Still, there was something familiar about the woman's build and the efficient way she moved. As if in slow motion, his gaze finally came to rest on her face.

Eyes he'd seen nearly every day of his life met his. Eyes the color of violets. Lips that had uttered his name a thousand times lifted—lips that were pink and full and the tiniest bit trembly.

Mel.

She smiled, so tremulously, so delicately his mouth went dry. Reverend Jones's voice was coming from someplace far away, but Clayt couldn't make out the words over the explosion in his head. His eyes strayed to the wisps of hair brushing Mel's eyebrows and the slightly longer tendrils grazing the base of her neck where her heavy braid used to be.

What the hell had she done to her hair?

He was vaguely aware that people were looking at him. And he thought he heard Reverend Jones clear his throat. But it was the repetitive movement of Mel's head that finally got through to Clayt. He glanced at Luke and Wyatt, who were looking at him strangely. Through the roaring din in his ears, he heard his brother say, "The rings, Clayt. We need the rings."

Clayt fumbled in his pockets, came up empty-handed, and fumbled again. By the time he'd given the proper rings to the right couple, the din in his ears had turned into a silent hush that was even more unsettling.

While Luke and Jillian, and Wyatt and Lisa, exchanged sacred vows and wedding rings, Clayt told himself he'd been imagining his reaction to Mel. To prove it, he cast another glance in her direction. For a moment he froze all over again. Everyone else in the church was looking at the brides and grooms. Mel was looking at him.

His mouth went slack, and the strangest sensation began to uncurl low in his belly. Somehow managing to tear his gaze away, he clamped his mouth shut and told himself to get a grip.

For crying out loud, that was Mel McCully. The girl who'd stuck her tongue out at him so often he'd lost count. The girl he'd teased incessantly when they were kids. The girl he'd caught with her grandfather's chewing tobacco when she was ten. The girl he'd never thought of as a girl at all.

Clayt rubbed his hand across his jaw. Luke and Wyatt were kissing their brides. And Clayt had the strangest urge to kiss Mel.

He was either going crazy, or he'd been without a woman for far too long. The way he saw it, that was enough to drive any hot-blooded man crazy. But Mel McCully? Nah.

It had to be the candles or the ever-darkening stained-glass windows or the occasion, or something. Hell, it could be anything, as long as it wasn't honest-to-goodness attraction.

"Well?" Jillian asked, reaching for a glass of punch. "Has my new brother-in-law noticed?"

"Details," Lisa whispered, her dark eyes dancing in her heart-shaped face. "We want details."

Mel finished ladling punch into another glass before taking a close look at her friends. Their gowns were as beautiful and unique as the personalities of the women wearing them. Jillian's was made of old-fashioned lace with pearl buttons down the back. It had a waist that dipped low in front, the material falling over her hips and legs like a whisper with every step she took. Lisa's gown was made of shiny satin and had a neckline just low enough to hint at the lush curves the bodice covered but couldn't hide. Her dress had short sleeves, the hem and waistline trimmed with thousands of tiny rhinestones.

"Are you going to keep us waiting all day?" Jillian prodded.

Mel handed a glass of punch to two young boys. When they were out of hearing range, she said, "He noticed."

"I knew it," Lisa exclaimed.

"What did he say?" Jillian asked.

"What did he do?" Lisa cut in.

Hooking the ladle on the side of the punch bowl, Mel grinned. "Well, he almost dropped your rings for one thing."

"So that's what that was all about," Jillian said.

"Ye-ha!" Lisa exclaimed. "You were right to keep the changes as subtle as possible, Mel. That man's staggering beneath the weight of a ton of bricks, and he doesn't even know what hit him."

"You could be right," Mel said around another smile.

"Has he said anything?" Jillian asked.

"Not exactly. He's been steering clear of me ever since the ceremony. But he's been watching me like a hawk."

Reaching up to adjust the flowers in her long, red hair, Jillian said, "He's more than likely trying to tell himself that he's imagining the whole thing. 'See?' he's probably saying to himself right now. 'Nothing's changed. She's manning the punch table just like she always does.'"

Feeling as if she were in a time warp that was a cross between Christmas morning and the first day of spring, Mel chanced a glance across the old town hall. Pretending that she hadn't noticed Clayt peering at her instead of looking at Brandy Schafer who obviously wanted his attention, she let Lisa and Jillian sweep her with them to the edge of the plank dance floor where their new husbands were waiting and the Anderson brothers were starting to play.

There. See? She manned the punch table just like she always does. There's nothing unusual about that or about Mel. It's all in your head, Carson.

Clayt rotated a kink out of his shoulders and released a deep breath. When he'd first seen the tendrils of hair skimming Mel's ears and neck he'd thought she'd gone and had her hair chopped off. Now he realized she was wearing it up, that was all. He wasn't accustomed to seeing Mel

McCully in that kind of dress, either, but Brandy Schafer had told him that Lisa was stocking a new style of women's wear in the Jasper Gulch Clothing Store. That pretty much explained the differences in Mel's appearance. Now that he knew that his initial reaction to her had been nothing more than a combination of surprise and a figment of his imagination, he could relax and enjoy the reception.

After checking on Haley, who was having a punch-drinking contest with Jeremy Everts, Clayt joined a group of ranchers who were complaining about the middle man and the shortage of hay and oats due to the summer's drought. He happened to glance at Mel while Grover Andrews was asking her to dance. All in all, Clayt thought it was right nice of her to give that mama's boy the time of day. It just went to show that Mel could be nice when she put her mind to it.

He was talking to Cletus when he noticed her dancing with Jason Tucker. Cletus snapped one suspender, and Clayt shook his head. That young buck loved to dance so much he'd been known to kick up his heels with his own great-grandmother.

Clayt was standing with his parents when Boomer Brown called for all the single gals to gather on the dance floor for the traditional tossing of the bouquet. "Look, son," Rita Carson said, laying a hand on Clayt's arm. "Haley's going to try to catch one of the bouquets."

Lisa and Jillian turned around at one end of the dance floor. All around them the folks of Jasper Gulch started counting backward. Ten. Clayt shook his head and gave his mother an indulgent smile. "I'm hoping to be a groom again before I become the father of the bride. That girl of mine has had me going around in circles all summer. Thank goodness you're home."

At the count of nine, Rita Carson glanced up at her oldest son and said, "Oh, didn't your father tell you?"

Clayt shook his head. "Tell me what?"

"We're going back to Oregon first thing Monday morning."

At seven Clayt narrowed his eyes at his father. Hugh Carson nodded and grinned. He'd been doing a lot of that since he'd gotten back from Oregon. Clayt wished he'd cut it out.

At six Rita said, "We wouldn't have missed your brother's wedding for the world. Your father and I are so proud of both you boys. I can hardly wait for Mama to be completely well so we can come home for good and get to know our new daughter-in-law."

At four Clayt scowled and said, "What about Haley?"

Three.

"She's adorable."

Two.

"And she certainly reminds me of you when you were that age."

One.

Looking up at her son, Rita exclaimed, "You'd better hurry if you want to be a groom again, Clayton, because Haley just caught Lisa's bouquet." Still laughing, she set off toward her only granddaughter.

Wondering if it might not be a good idea to simply lock his daughter in the attic until she turned thirty, Clayt leaned against the wall. On the other side of the dance floor Boomer Brown was taking a lot of elbow jabbing over the fact that DoraLee had caught the other bouquet. Sparing a glance at his father, Clayt said, "You're really not home to stay?"

Hugh Carson was the same height as his sons, but his hair had turned gray and his face bore the lines of all the years he'd spent out on the range. Staring across the room at the woman he'd married nearly forty years ago, he said, "When I met your mother I didn't think a thing of whisking her away from Oregon and everybody and everything she knew. She's already lost your grandpa, but it looks as if your grandma's going to pull through. The time your mother is spending back there now is giving her a chance to get reacquainted with the friends she knew growing up. You can handle the ranch on your own, son. Something tells me you can handle Haley, too.''

Clayt figured he should have thanked his father for the vote of confidence, but Mel swung by on Rory O'Grady's arm, and whatever he'd been about to say died on his lips. The O'Gradys owned the largest spread in this part of South Dakota and never passed up the opportunity to brag about it. If you asked Clayt, Rory's hair was a little too black, his pants a little too tight, his clothes a little too flashy right down to his snakeskin boots.

The lighting in the old town hall had never been great, but Clayt could see the intent in Rory's eyes all the way from here. The fact that Rory was a self-acclaimed ladies' man didn't bother Clayt. But when Mel reached up on tiptoe to hear what Rory was whispering in her ear, Clayt clenched his teeth so hard his jaw ached.

"Is it just me?" Hugh asked, "or is there something different about Mel McCully tonight?"

Before Clayt could add anything to his snort, Rory whisked Mel away in the other direction. Folks started clapping their hands and stomping their feet as other couples headed for the floor. Mel and Rory didn't seem to notice. Clayt didn't wholly recognize the feeling creeping under his skin but he didn't like it one bit.

Emerging from the crowd, Boomer Brown sidled up next to him and crossed his arms at his massive chest. "Jed Winters mentioned that Grover Andrews told him that Karl Hanson claims that Mel said she finally realizes how silly her infatuation with you has been all these years. I never would have believed it if I hadn't seen her dancing with Rory with my own two eyes.''

Slapping his son on the back, Hugh Carson said, ''Well, well, well. What do you think about that?''

Rory dipped Mel, the action drawing attention to the smooth column of her throat and the soft-looking skin visible above the scooped neckline of her dress. Watching through narrowed eyes, heat started in Clayt's chest, only to twist and turn and slowly burrow lower.

What did he think? his father had asked.

Clayt thought that woman was making a spectacle of herself. And by God, something had to be done.

Chapter Three

The clock on Main Street struck midnight as Clayt cut across the alley and yanked on the door that led to Mel's place. The wedding reception was finally over. A person would think the folks of Jasper Gulch had never been to a wedding before. They sure hadn't been in any hurry to leave. As far as Clayt was concerned the whole thing should have ended right after Luke, Jillian, Wyatt and Lisa had left for their honeymoons. The longer it had dragged on, the more disgusted he'd become.

The light was off in the stairway below Mel's place, but he didn't bother searching for the switch. He, Luke and Wyatt had sneaked up there so often when they were kids he could have found his way blindfolded. The apartment had been vacant back then, which had made it the perfect place to steal a kiss from Angela Nelson after the homecoming dance when he was sixteen. He hadn't been up here much since he'd helped Wyatt and Cletus move Mel's things in when she bought the diner ten years ago, but the lack of good lighting didn't slow him down. He had a bone to pick with Mel McCully, and the sooner he got it over with the sooner things could get back to normal around here.

The thought of Mel grated on his nerves. There was nothing unusual about that. Hell, she'd been like fingernails on a chalkboard for as long as he could remember. Holding that thought, he reached for the doorknob. At the last minute he raised his fist and knocked instead.

"Come on in. The door's open."

Gearing up to say what was on his mind, he stormed inside. He opened his mouth to speak, only to clamp it shut again when he found himself alone in the room.

"I'm a little surprised Boomer dropped you off so early, DoraLee," Mel called, her voice coming from someplace down the hall. "You must be as anxious to talk about the wedding as I am. Make yourself comfortable. I'll be right out."

Clayt had never been very good at waiting, and he'd already been waiting hours to speak his mind. After striding to the window overlooking Main Street, he glanced around the room. The apartment wasn't large. He could see most of it from here. A kitchen too small to turn around in was completely dark, but light spilled from a narrow hallway on the right. There was gray carpeting on the living room floor, a blue sofa on one wall, a television on another and a lamp turned to its lowest setting in the far corner. The coffee table was cluttered; the wicker basket beside it literally overflowed with magazines and newspapers. Mel McCully had never been much of a neat freak, that was for sure.

Clayt had no idea why that thought made him feel better, but suddenly he figured it wouldn't hurt to take a seat. He was in the process of pushing an old afghan and a pile of clothes out of his way on the sofa when he caught a movement out of the corner of his eye.

Mel entered the room talking, her hands fiddling with a clasp in her hair. "So, DoraLee, what did Boomer say about the fact that you caught the bouquet?"

Her hair fell around her shoulders just as her gaze met his. She *had* cut her hair.

"You're not DoraLee."

Feeling like a deer trapped in the glare of headlights, Clayt could only shake his head.

"What are you doing here?" she asked.

He straightened and tried to speak, but had to clear his throat and try a second time. "I came to talk to you."

She pushed her hair away from her face, then let her fingers trail through the ends as if she wasn't accustomed to its new length, either. "Oh. Okay. What did you want to talk to me about?"

He almost tripped over her shoes as he took a step, which made him glance down at her stockinged feet, which drew his gaze over the peach-colored fabric of her skirt and on up to a waist that looked amazingly narrow. Higher, the fabric ended at the creamy expanse of skin he'd never paid much attention to until Rory O'Grady had bent her over his arm earlier.

Suddenly seething with renewed anger, he narrowed his eyes and gave his head a hard nod. "What the hell were you trying to do tonight?"

Mel took a calming breath. Honestly, it required an iron will to keep from telling Clayt to take a flying leap. *That* was what the old Mel would have done. The new Mel pretended not to notice how good he looked with his collar unbuttoned and his dress slacks slung low on his hips. The new Mel looked into his eyes and ever-so-innocently asked, "What do you mean?"

She could tell her question threw him, but being a Carson, which meant that he was quick-witted, among other things, he recovered almost immediately. "I mean it wasn't a good idea to let every bachelor in the county see you twirling around the dance floor with the biggest womanizer in South Dakota—especially looking the way you looked tonight. I don't know what you were trying to prove, but I don't think—"

The step Mel took toward him stopped him in the middle of his tirade. "What's wrong with the way I look?"

Clayt swallowed. Hard. What was wrong with the way she looked? The long plain braid was gone, for one thing. Now her hair waved almost to her shoulders as if it had a mind of its own. Not that he should have been surprised about that. But he'd never noticed those golden highlights before, and he was certain her eyes used to be plain blue, not violet. When had she grown those eyelashes? And those lips. Those pink, full, wet lips.

"Clayt?"

He came to in slow motion. Where was he? Oh, yeah. Taking inventory of what was wrong with Wyatt's little sister. Only Mel wasn't little anymore. At least not every-where. He remembered the summer she'd started wearing a bra. He and Wyatt had teased the living daylights out of her. Back then she'd been as skinny as a cat in a bath. She was still skinny. Almost. It was that *almost* that made him pause, because where she wasn't skinny she was damned appealing.

What was wrong with the way she looked? he asked himself as his gaze made its way back the way it had come, over narrow hips, gently sloping breasts, the shadow in the little hollow at the base of her neck, to her lips. Those pink, full, wet lips.

He swallowed again, but it only made him aware of the pulsing sensation in his throat and the growing pressure much, much lower. "People are talking," he declared.

"The people of Jasper Gulch always talk."

"Yes, but do you want them to whisper about you behind their hands and brand you a..."

Holding up a hand, she took another step toward him. "Before you call me a hussy, I believe you have my slip."

He glanced down at the scrap of lace and satin he must have picked up without realizing it when he'd been trying to clear a spot to sit down. Aware of how he must look fingering her underclothes, he clenched his jaw. He was all ready to set her straight when she tugged on the slip, causing it to swish over his wrist and wind through his fingers like a whisper slipping through a sigh.

He rubbed his fingers over his palm and found himself looking in a place he had no business looking. Feeling guilty and agitated, he tore his gaze away from Mel's breasts and glanced around the room once again. He'd noticed the clutter before. Why hadn't he noticed how feminine the room was? The garden prints on the wall, the light gray carpet on the floor and the sky blue couch weren't exactly frilly, but they were *womanly*. Funny. Until today he'd never thought of Mel in exactly that way.

"You were saying?" she asked quietly.

A force bigger than him drew him closer. Mmm, he thought, inhaling her scent. "Since when do you wear perfume?"

"Do you like it?"

His gaze got stuck on her mouth all over again. He'd always thought Mel's smile was too big for her face. Tonight, it didn't seem too big at all. Her lips were full, yes, but not too full. They looked perfect.

Perfect for kissing.

"Clayt?"

When had her voice become sultry? And when, exactly, had he lost his mind? He ran a hand through his hair and pulled himself together. Good God, this was Mel McCully. What in the world was he thinking? Clenching his teeth, he sputtered, "What difference does it make if I like it? The question you should be asking yourself is whether or not you want to have the reputation of a floozy."

She plunked her hands on her hips and raised her chin the way she'd been doing all her life. "Clayt Carson, you couldn't say something nice if your life depended on it."

Clayt's vision cleared. And then he did something he hadn't done since he'd caught sight of Mel during the wedding ceremony hours ago. He grinned. This was more like it. This Mel he could handle.

"Would you mind telling me why you cut your hair and why you're wearing makeup?" he asked, the epitome of superior rationality.

"I took Granddad's advice," she said.

"Cletus had something to do with this?"

Try as he might, Clayt couldn't help noticing the way the light shimmered over her hair when she nodded. She tossed the slip to the sofa and turned, her skirt brushing his pant leg. He had a hard time swallowing.

From the other side of the room, she said, "He says a person catches more bees with honey."

"Since when have you been interested in catching bees?"

He didn't like the way she shrugged, or the way she turned, or the way he was reacting to the sight of either of those things. "Not bees, Clayt. I'm trying to draw a man."

"Rory O'Grady?"

"Pu-lease."

Clayt admitted that he wasn't entirely comfortable with the turn his hormones had taken, but he was enjoying the smug feeling of satisfaction coursing through him right now. Mel had gone to a lot of trouble to impress somebody, and it hadn't been Rory O'Grady. Hot dang, he hadn't lost his touch after all. Not that he'd ever *really* doubted it.

Mel was meandering on the other side of the room, letting her hand trail over the top of the television, along a windowsill and onto a picture frame of her parents, taken a long time ago. Doing his best to hold back a grin, he said, "So you've done all this to try to impress a man other than Rory."

She shrugged again and answered without turning around. "I'm not getting any younger, you know."

"Then you see marriage in your future?"

She nodded, and Clayt was almost glad she wasn't looking, because he couldn't keep the hundred-watt grin off his face no matter how hard he tried. "Then why don't you just end this stupid charade and marry me once and for all?"

"What?"

When she turned this time, his mouth went dry for an entirely different reason. "Look, Mel, that didn't sound quite the way I intended."

Mel's hair may have been shorter, and she might have been wearing a dress he hadn't seen until today, but he recognized the daggers shooting from her eyes, and nobody else could twist their upper lip in such a snide way or sputter quite so vehemently.

"Stupid charade? You think this was all for your pathetic benefit? And people say Rory's got a big head. I said I wanted a man, Clayt. I didn't say I wanted you. I wouldn't marry an arrogant, muddleheaded ignoramus like you if you were the last man on earth."

He knew she couldn't possibly reach him from the other side of the room, but Clayt took a step backward anyway. He bit back a curse and sputtered, "I don't know why I bothered."

"*Don't* bother," she taunted as he strode to the door. "And the next time you get the urge to fondle women's lingerie, I suggest you buy your own!"

Fondle women's lingerie? He hadn't been fondling...

She slammed the door so hard Clayt doubted his ears would ever be the same. He took to the steps like a man being chased by a demon. By the time he reached the bottom, he figured that was a pretty good description of the hothead upstairs. He was still sputtering when he stomped into the alley and headed for his truck.

Confounded, contrary, ill-tempered, cantankerous woman.

Mel McCully hadn't changed. She hadn't changed at all.

"I've changed, haven't I, Granddad?" Mel asked, handing a wet plate to Cletus.

"Oh, I s'pose there have been a few..."

Up to her elbows in soapy water, Mel pushed her hair away from her cheek with her shoulder and forged ahead in the middle of her grandfather's reply. "I admit that I miss the convenience of my braid, but I don't miss its weight or the way it looked. And what's wrong with wearing a pretty dress once in my life? And there isn't any law against using a little lipstick and mascara."

Accustomed as he was to these talk sessions, when Mel didn't let him get a word in edgewise, Cletus simply nodded. Scrubbing another plate, Mel said, "Clayt thinks he knows who I am. He thinks he can barge into my place and ask me what I'm trying to prove. If he didn't have such a thick skull he'd know I'm not trying to *prove* anything. I'm trying to show him something."

"He got your dander up, did he?" Cletus asked.

Mel shrugged one shoulder as she thought about a few of the things she'd said the night before last. For heaven's sake, she'd practically called Clayt a pervert. Handing her grandfather another plate, she said, "I might have uttered a word or two I shouldn't have."

Pursing his thin lips, Cletus said, "Oh-oh. What did you say?"

"Well, I seem to recall mentioning that I wouldn't marry an arrogant, muddleheaded ignoramus like him if he were the last man on earth."

Cletus shook his old head. "I thought you were going to hold your temper where Clayt's concerned from now on."

Mel leaned on the old sink, suddenly tired. "It could take me the rest of my life to learn to hold on to my temper where Clayt is concerned. I wanted him to notice me, and I ended up making him mad just like I always do. I'm a pathetic, hopeless spinster who will be thirty in a few months. At this rate he'll never notice me."

"You said he *did* notice you, girl. Besides, I don't want you to change too much. I'm a mite partial to you just the way you are."

Leave it to her grandfather to say the only thing in the world that could have made her feel better. Smiling, she reached through the soapsuds for a saucer. Granddad was right. She wanted to make a few changes in her life, but she didn't want to become someone else.

The diner had been closed yesterday just as it always was on Sundays. Mel had spent a good share of her day off wandering through the empty rooms, lost in thought. Mel's Diner wasn't big, but it was clean and the food was decent. The place had ten tables, eight booths, and a hat rack by the door. The faded awning outside matched the faded checkered curtains at the front window. Nobody seemed to mind. Folks came to the diner for food and gossip, not ambience.

Mel was proud of her diner. She truly enjoyed what she did for a living. She just didn't want it to be her whole life.

"I want a man to love, Granddad, and maybe a baby or two. I'm a normal woman with a normal woman's needs. Why is that so impossible for Clayt to fathom?"

"You have to remember who you're dealing with here.

Clayt's a Carson, and the Carsons are a bit more difficult than most men. He thinks he knows who you are.''

"He knows what he sees, but he's never actually seen all the way to my heart.''

"Then you're going to have to find a way to open his eyes. It worked Saturday night, didn't it?''

Mel reached to the bottom of the sink for a handful of silverware, thinking that Cletus had a point. Clayt had noticed her at the wedding two days ago. She couldn't have been mistaken about that. He'd noticed the changes in her appearance, and *she'd* noticed his reaction to them. She may not have had much experience with men, but even she'd been able to tell that Clayt Carson had been attracted to her. He was just fighting it with everything he had.

That was one of the things Mel hoped to change. Glancing over her shoulder at the dishes still waiting to be washed, she knew she had to make a few changes in the diner, too. The local folks liked her home-cooked meals, but the shortage of women in the area had left her short-handed. Her best waitress had moved to Pierre three months ago. Now that Lisa was married and her clothing store was becoming a success she wouldn't have time to work the supper crowd anymore. DoraLee helped out now and then, and Cletus did what he could. But it wasn't enough. She needed a waitress who knew how to cook and wasn't afraid to wash dishes on a daily basis. Men in other parts of the United States became waiters, but here in Jasper Gulch they still considered waiting tables women's work.

The sound of the bell jingling over the front door had Mel glancing at the clock. It was only three in the afternoon. The lunch rush was over and the supper crowd didn't normally start to filter in until four-thirty. Drying her hands on a towel, she said, "Guess I'd better go see who that is.''

"Take this with you," Cletus said, handing her the Help

Wanted sign lying on the counter. "I don't mind peeling potatoes, but the other day Doc Masey accused me of having dishpan hands. I might not be as young as I used to be, but I've still got a reputation to protect."

Smiling at the man who had raised her, Mel said, "Come on, Granddad, you're as young as you feel and you know it."

Cletus snapped one suspender and grimaced. "If that's true I'm in big trouble. My rheumatiz is actin' up, my hearing ain't what it used to be, and just last night Roy Everts beat me at poker for the first time in fifteen years. I don't mind gettin' old. I just wish it wasn't so dang painful."

Looking into her grandfather's craggy face, Mel had a feeling that he was a lot more upset about the poker game than sore joints or a loss of hearing. After planting a kiss on his lined cheek, she headed for the dining room, sign in hand.

"Mel?" Cletus called, stopping her in the doorway. "Maybe you should apologize to Clayt for callin' him names. That would certainly surprise the living daylights out of him. And when you're finished, maybe you should plant a kiss on his cheek like the one you just whispered on mine. If that don't shock the patooty out of him, nothing will."

Unsure whether to shrug or grimace, Mel continued on into the dining room, only to come to an abrupt stop on the other side of the swinging door. The bell *had* jangled, but no one was there. Nobody had sidled up to the counter or taken a seat at a booth or table. Deciding that stranger things had happened, she strolled toward the window to hang the sign, lost in thought.

Her grandfather was probably right about apologizing to Clayt. Too bad apologizing ranked right up there with washing another sink-load of dishes. Maybe she should wait until Clayt came into the diner again. Of course, after the things she'd said Saturday night that probably wouldn't be anytime soon. But kiss him? She'd been waiting all her life for him to kiss *her*.

She was in the process of calling herself a coward when she heard a scuffing sound on the other side of the room. Peering into the shadows beneath the booths, she caught sight of a tennis shoe and a little girl's light brown hair.

"Haley, is that you?"

Haley Carson muttered an unbecoming word.

"I got my mouth washed out for saying that, when I was your age. It isn't a very nice word, you know. If you've ever gotten any on your shoe, you know why."

The child sighed.

Squatting down so she could see beneath the bench, Mel said, "Might as well say you're sorry and get it over with."

"Do I hafta?" Haley's voice sounded very small.

"It ain't easy, believe me, I know. But yes, Haley, you have to."

"Sorry."

"That's better," Mel said. "Now, what are you doing under my booth?"

"Nothin'."

"Haley."

"I missed the bus?"

"I see." Not that Mel believed her. "In that case, do you want a ride home?"

"Not really."

"Why not?"

"Do I need a reason?"

Mel gave the girl a stern look, but secretly she was relieved to hear the rising vehemence in the little waif's voice. "Around here you do," Mel answered. "You might as well explain it to me after you crawl out from under there."

"I'd rather explain it from here."

"I'd rather you didn't. Come on. Out."

Haley squirmed her way out like a contortionist at a carnival sideshow. Climbing to her feet, she took a minute to straighten her shirt and jeans. Mel noticed she didn't bother to push her hair out of her face. "I don't wanna go home just yet," she said, inordinately intrigued with the toe of her shoe.

"Why is that?"

"Clayton's not gonna be very happy to see me."

"I don't think that's true, Haley."

"He's gonna be mad at me."

Mel waited for the child to continue. It looked as if she might be in for a long wait. Deciding a little prodding was in order, Mel said, "Why might your father be mad at you?"

"It might be a lot of things."

Mel raised her eyebrows and lowered her chin.

"Oh, all right. He's gonna be mad at me cuz I sort of got in a fight at school."

What was it with the Carsons and *sort of?*

Mel took Haley's chin in her fingers and gently lifted. The girl was going to be a looker some day, but not until her black eye healed.

"Does that hurt?" Mel asked.

"Not as much as Bobby's split lip."

If the situation hadn't been so serious, Mel might have smiled at the little girl's pluck. She'd never much cared for Victoria Carson, but she had to hand it to the woman for passing on the right genes to her only child. Haley had her mother's bone structure, and when her eye wasn't swollen shut, she had her mother's pretty features. Thank goodness Victoria had hoarded all her selfishness to herself.

Sighing the way she did whenever she thought of Clayt's ex-wife, Mel said, "Your father's going to want to know who started it."

"You think?"

Mel nodded. "I've known him a lot longer than you have. Believe me, he's gonna want to know. *Did* Bobby throw the first punch?"

The child's gaze went back to the toe of her shoe as she said, "Not exactly."

"So you hit him first."

"He had it coming."

"There are a lot of people in the world who have it coming, Haley. Unfortunately, we can't go around beating them all up."

Haley only shrugged.

Glancing over her shoulder where a horrendous noise had just erupted from the kitchen, Mel said, "My grandfather's doing dishes. If I play my cards right and you let me take you home, they could all be done by the time I get back."

Heaving a sigh bigger than she was, Haley said, "I guess."

"Come on. My car's parked in the alley. We can cut through the kitchen, tell Granddad where we're going and grab some ice for your eye."

"Mel?" Haley asked before they'd taken three steps. "Will you tell Clayton for me?"

Staring at Haley's earnest expression, Mel said, "Bobby really had it coming?"

Haley nodded solemnly.

"I'll tell your father on one condition."

It was amazing how suspicious a ragamuffin nine-year-old girl with a swollen eye and wrinkled clothes could look. "What condition?"

"I'll explain things to your father if you agree to help me out in the diner."

Haley's good eye opened wide. "You mean like a job?"

Mel nodded.

"Would I get paid?"

"You do the job, you earn the pay."

"Yippee! When can I start?"

"Tomorrow right after school. We'll need your father's permission," Mel said around a smile.

"He'll let me. Come on, Mel. Hurry and take me home."

Clayt was in the corral with one of the horses when Mel and Haley pulled into the driveway. Although Haley tried to hide her ice pack, Mel was pretty sure he knew something was going on. Not much got past Clayt Carson. Except *her* all these years, that is.

Haley scampered into the house. By the time Mel had reached the corral, Clayt had removed his riding gloves with his teeth and was waiting for her, forearms resting on the gate, one boot hiked on a low board.

"How bad is it?" he asked, tipping his well-worn brown Stetson higher on his forehead.

Assuming a similar stance a few feet farther down the gate where General Custer, the best cattle dog Clayt had ever had was sprawled out in the sun, Mel said, "Remember the black eye Luke gave you for clipping his favorite horse's tail when you were twelve?"

Clayt grimaced. "That bad?"

Mel nodded. "She'll heal. How did you know she had a black eye?"

"I got a call from the principal fifteen minutes ago. Good old Mrs. Ferguson," he said.

"Yeah." Mel took in the grayed and weathered outbuildings, the straight fences and the lane that disappeared over the rolling hills on Carson land. Two white houses sat near the road, a hundred yards apart. Clayt and Haley lived in one, and as soon as Rita Carson finished nursing her mother back to health, she and Hugh would come back to the other. Everyone in town knew the story of how Jasper Carson,

Clayt's great-great-grandfather, founded the town more than a hundred years ago. Mel knew Clayt's life stories, and he knew hers. Unfortunately, she didn't know how to tell him she'd call back the words she'd shouted at him Saturday night if only she could.

"Thanks for bringing Haley home."

She turned her head and found Clayt looking at her. Normally his eyes appeared gunmetal gray. Today they were closer to the color of smoke. It didn't look as if he'd shaved since the wedding. It didn't look as if he'd slept a whole lot, either. An apology from her might make things a little better.

The horse nickered, and a cool wind ruffled through her hair and shirt. His boot scraped the bottom board as he pulled it off the gate and took a backward step. "Guess I'd better be getting back to work."

Mel called herself every kind of fool. No wonder Clayt didn't care about her. She couldn't even do something as simple and honorable as apologize.

"Clayt?"

He settled his hands on his hips and waited for her to continue. She was all set to simply say "I'm sorry," but try as she might, she couldn't get the words past her lips, and ended up saying, "I told Haley she could work at the diner as long as it's okay with you. She's got an active mind, and I think it might be a good idea to keep her as busy as possible..."

Clayt shook his head and gave Mel a grudging smile. For a second there he'd thought she was going to apologize for yelling at him Saturday night. Mel McCully could make a mean pot roast and a mouth-watering apple pie. She could wield a broom and ride a horse. She could even dance. But she'd never been worth a hill of beans at apologizing.

Her hair might have been different, but the rest of her

was the same as it had always been. That sameness was as comfortable as wool socks and flannel sheets.

Gradually he realized that Mel was still talking. "So, if it's all right with you, I thought I could have her stop in after school and wash dishes and maybe help me clean up before the supper crowd starts moseying in."

Clayt grinned again. Yup. As comfortable as wool socks, that's what she was. "That'll be fine, Mel. I think you might be on to something here."

Her genuine look of surprise made him realize how seldom he actually said something nice to her, let alone something complimentary. "Well," she said, leaning down to scratch the dog's head. "I guess I'd better be getting back to the diner."

"Okay, Mel. Thanks again for bringing Haley home."

"You're welcome, but that reminds me. My name is Melody."

"I know what your name is."

The wind blew her hair across her cheek, fluttering wisps into her eyes. Pushing them away with both hands, she said, "You don't understand. From now on I'd prefer to be called Melody. Not Mel."

Without another word, she turned on her heel and strode toward her car. Clayt's mouth went dry. Try as he might, he couldn't take his eyes off her. Her jeans had probably been washed a hundred times. They bagged a little in the seat, but it didn't detract from the feminine sway of her hips. That telltale need began to uncurl deep inside him again. When she glanced over her shoulder and caught him looking, he couldn't bring himself to move.

"Is something wrong?" she asked.

He shook his head.

They stared at each other, him inside the corral, her in the middle of the driveway. Just when he was beginning to wonder if they'd both lost the ability to speak, she said, "I'm sorry for what I said the other night."

"You are?"

She nodded. "I know you're not a pervert. And I shouldn't have called you an arrogant, muddleheaded ignoramus."

"Yeah?" he asked hoarsely.

"Yeah," she said, smiling. "You aren't really muddleheaded at all."

Clayt didn't know what to do about her wink, or about the freight train that was chugging through his chest. He was still standing in the middle of the corral trying to figure it all out when she drove away.

Something wrong, Clayt? she'd asked him.

Shoving his hands into his gloves, it seemed that the same things that were wrong with Mel, or, he grimaced, with *Melody,* were the same things that were right. He didn't know how the hell that had happened. And he sure didn't know what he was supposed to do about it.

General Custer wagged his tail, turned in a circle, then plopped to the ground in a warm patch of sun.

"Some help you are," Clayt grumbled.

The General closed his eyes and began to snore. The filly Clayt had been trying to break for Haley nickered behind him. Glancing from the horse, whose ears were laid back stubbornly, to the house where he still had to deal with Haley's latest escapades, to the road where Mel's car was barely visible, he did what he always did when faced with opposition or uncertainty of any kind. He crammed his hat on his head, dug in his heels and got to work.

Chapter Four

"Okay, Butch. I'll be here all morning. You can deliver those timbers anytime." After hanging up the phone, Clayt propped his feet on the coffee table, pointed the remote at the television and settled back to watch the late news.

"Mama says it's uncouth to put your feet on the coffee table."

He glanced at the stairway where his daughter was peering at him from between two spindles. Lowering his feet to the floor, he took in the cold lift of Haley's chin and the glower in her good eye. "Why aren't you sleeping?"

She answered with a dramatic shrug.

His daughter had always been a night owl, but she was usually more talkative than this. Which meant that she was holding a grudge because he'd made her apologize to Bobby Gentry for starting that fight. So far neither of the kids had come clean with the reason the fight broke out in the first place. Clayt knew from experience that if Haley chose not to tell, she never would.

Sliding down to the next step, she pulled her flannel

nightgown over her feet. After another tense moment of silence, she said, "I heard the phone."

"It was Butch. He's going to deliver some posts and timbers so I can start mending fences before the snow flies."

"Oh. I thought it might be Mama."

Clayt turned the television down with one hand and ran the other through his shower-damp hair. "No, Haley, it wasn't her."

"She'll call as soon as she finds herself."

He wondered how a woman who stared in a mirror as much as Victoria could possibly be lost, but he didn't say it out loud. Haley had stopped believing in Santa Claus two years ago, but she clung to her belief in Victoria, and Clayt just didn't have the heart to tell his daughter the truth about the mother she adored.

"Hey, Clayton?"

He'd never been able to understand why Haley insisted upon calling *him* Clayton while she called the woman who'd dumped her on his doorstep and had driven away without a backward glance Mama.

"What's yellow and smells like bananas?"

She'd made her way to the bottom step, her expression one of fledgling contrition. He pursed his lips and placed his chin in his hand as if giving the question a great deal of thought. "Yellow and smells like bananas, huh? I have no idea."

"Monkey puke."

Clayt's chuckle came out of the blue and rumbled in his chest like the purr of a big cat. Sensing that all was forgiven, Haley went down another step. With a hop, skip and a jump she was beside him on the couch.

"Did you hear that in school?" he asked.

"Nope," she said, wiggling closer, "Mel told me."

That sounded like Mel, Clayt thought as he tucked an

afghan around Haley. Suddenly chatty, his daughter said, "Mel—I mean Melody—told me she'll pay me twenty-five cents over minimum wage for washing dishes. Fifty if the spoons are so clean she can see herself in them. She's nice."

Mel McCully. Nice? Clayt had never thought of her that way, but he supposed Haley was right. Mel really was nice to everybody except him.

Listening with only one ear as Haley began to talk about everything from the half-grown kittens that lived in the barn to the filly she'd chosen as her own, he made a mental note to thank Mel for knowing what his little girl needed and offering it to her in a way that left her ego intact. Mel, er, Melody, or whatever the heck he was supposed to call her now, really was a good sport. She was also very good with kids. Even Haley liked her, and she didn't like just anybody. Maybe he should rethink his strategy where Mel was concerned. After all, even Cletus had said a person could attract more bees with honey.

Haley had begun to slow down when the weatherman claimed the screen, and she'd completely run out of steam by the time the news was over. He punched the Power button on the remote before carrying his sleeping daughter up to bed, where he tucked the blankets under her chin.

Tiptoeing down the stairs, he wondered why he hadn't thought of being *nice* to Mel before. If she'd always had a crush on him when he'd teased her, imagine what would happen if he actually treated her nicely.

Be nice to Mel McCully. What an unusual concept.

Grinning, he shrugged out of his T-shirt and sank to the edge of his bed. Hot dang, this was going to be a snap. A piece of cake. As easy as one, two, three.

It was after eight when he knocked on Mel's door the following night. This time the light was on in the stairway, and while he still could have found his way in the dark, tonight he wasn't the least bit angry.

Her smile slipped the tiniest bit when she opened the door and found him standing on her doorstep. "I don't have any coffee, Clayt."

He figured he deserved that. Determined to show her just how *nice* he could be, he gave her his slowest grin and removed his hat. "I didn't come here for coffee."

"You didn't?"

"Can't a man drop in on a woman without wanting coffee?"

He heard the little catch in her throat and saw her lips part in surprise. Earlier, he'd tried to remember how long it had been since he'd put his charms to work and actively pursued a woman. He'd even harbored the fleeting thought that he might be a little rusty. Smiling to himself now, he realized he needn't have worried. It was like riding a bike. Once a man knew how, he never forgot.

"Mind if I come in, Mel?"

She looked at him as if she plain didn't know what to do with his *nice* side. Clayt didn't blame her, but when she finally stepped to one side and motioned him in, he had to admit he was enjoying this very much.

He strode to the center of the small room, tossed his hat on the coffee table, and slowly turned around. The afghan was folded neatly over the back of the sofa, the clean laundry was gone, and he could see the tracks the vacuum cleaner had left in the carpet. "The place looks good."

She fluffed a pillow on the couch before pointing to the only closet in the room. "Whatever you do, don't open that door."

He rocked back on his heels and smiled down at her. "You clean like I do."

Without looking at him, she began to straighten the magazines lying on the low table. "The diner doesn't leave me much time for anything other than the bare necessities."

Clayt had noticed the Help Wanted sign in the diner's front window, but until now he hadn't given much thought to the amount of work it required to keep the place going. No wonder he rarely saw her sitting still.

"Mel," he said, covering her hand with his own.

She glanced up at him in surprise, the low drone of the television the only thing covering the silence stretching between them. It reminded him of how many things he and Mel had in common. He used to keep a television or radio playing in an otherwise empty house, too. Of course, now he had Haley. Which was why he was here.

He was growing accustomed to the blue of Mel's eyes, the curl of her lashes and the paleness of her skin, but the heat pooling low in his body still came as a bit of a surprise. Not that he minded. Hell, he couldn't think of anything he enjoyed more than the need of a man for a woman.

Mel felt frozen, unsure what to do or say. Until Saturday night Clayt hadn't set foot inside her apartment once in all the years she'd lived here. Suddenly he'd dropped by twice in one week. His jacket was open, the collar turned up, his blue shirt a pale contrast to his tanned skin and dark brown hair. She'd always claimed he was too tall to talk to. She had the strangest feeling that he hadn't stopped by to talk.

"Clayt..."

"You know," he said, interrupting her. "I like your hair this way."

"You do?"

"You sound surprised. What's the matter? Hasn't a man ever told you you're pretty?"

Her throat had closed so tight she could only whisper. "Granddad has, but you've always said I was as ordinary as quack grass."

"That wasn't very nice of me, was it? What else has your grandfather told you?"

Swallowing, Melody said, "He told me a kiss on the cheek surprises the patooty out of most men."

"Were you thinking about trying it on me?"

She opened her mouth to speak, but couldn't form a single word. His face blurred before her eyes as he moved closer, his voice a husky rasp in her ear as he said, "I have a better idea, Mel."

His lips found hers the way lightning found the ground. He seemed a little surprised by it, but not too surprised to keep from wrapping his arms around her back and drawing her up as if she weighed no more than a feather. His chin rasped her cheek, his breath mingling with hers. His arms felt like heaven, his kiss slow and hungry and deep. She'd been dreaming of this moment all her life, but Clayt Carson in the flesh was beyond her wildest fantasies.

When they'd both used up all the air in their lungs, the kiss broke. Instead of drawing away, Clayt kissed her cheek, her temple, her jaw. "Now will you say you'll marry me?" he asked, his voice a husky murmur.

She let her head fall back, her eyes opening as if in slow motion. Mmm, her mind was hazy, her body as weightless as a cloud. "I can't marry you, Clayt," she whispered. "I have a date."

"You have a what?" he asked, nuzzling her hair away from her ear.

The knock on the door cleared her mind and brought her to her senses. Pulling away slightly, she said, "I have a date. That's him now."

"You have a date?" Clayt's arms fell away from Mel's back, his hands squeezing into fists at his sides. "You kissed me as if there were no tomorrow, knowing full well that you were going on a date any minute?"

For a moment she looked lost and bewildered. Before

his eyes, that changed. She swung around, planted her hands on her hips and raised her chin at that haughty angle she'd perfected when she was six. "*I* didn't kiss *you,* Clayt Carson. You kissed me. I had no idea you were coming over tonight. If you had bothered to call first, I would have told you I was busy."

Clayt knew she had a point, dammit, but he wasn't ready to cease and desist. Returning the daggers she'd just shot at him, he let his lip curl snidely as he sputtered, "I went through a lot of trouble to be nice to you tonight. I mended fences on the ranch all day. For Haley's sake I thought I should try to mend a few with you. And this is the thanks I get."

At a complete and utter loss for anything to say, Melody could only stare at Clayt, her eyes wide, her mouth gaping, her thoughts pummeling her mind at breakneck speed. She'd been waiting for this man all her life. And tonight he'd finally come here, finally kissed her. She'd thought he was seeing her as a woman he could love. But it had all been a precalculated ploy to find a mother for Haley. He didn't care about her any more today than he had a month ago, a year ago or ten.

Melody McCully was a fool.

A knock sounded again. Glancing over her shoulder, she called, "I'll be right there, Ben."

Ben? Clayt thought to himself. She was going on a date with Ben Jacobs?

Suddenly the clean apartment, the faint traces of makeup, her Western skirt and the deep purple shirt he didn't remember seeing before made sense. She hadn't dressed up for him. She'd done it because she had a date.

She strode to the center of the room, turned around and squared off opposite him. They stared each other down. He caught a glimpse of her anger. Deep down he caught a glimpse of her hurt, as well. Hell. He felt like a heel. He was in the process of taking a step toward her when she held up one hand, halting his forward motion.

"Don't," she said. "Just don't." Smoothing her hands down her clothes, she took a deep breath and opened the door.

"Hi, Ben. Come on in."

"Hi, Mel-o-dy. Don't you look nice."

Clayt cringed at the male appreciation in Ben Jacobs's voice. When Ben managed to peel his eyes off Mel, Clayt cringed even more at the surprise. "Hey, Clayt. What are you doing here?"

He managed a civil greeting, but it took a long time for the explosion to recede inside his skull. Ben Jacobs was a thirty-year-old bachelor with a good head on his shoulders and a friendly disposition. At the moment, Clayt couldn't think of a living soul he disliked more.

Reading the warning in Mel's eyes, he drew in another deep breath and said, "Can't seem to find anybody else who can make coffee as thick as tar the way Mel can."

Mel flashed Clayt another stern look. "Clayt was just leaving." Turning to Ben, she said, "I'll be with you as soon as I grab my coat."

The instant she headed for her bedroom, Clayt reached for his hat and made a beeline for the door.

"Clayt, wait up a minute," Ben called.

Clayt didn't have a minute, because in a minute he was going to explode. Holding on to his temper by the skin of his teeth, he faced Ben. The other man shifted from one foot to the other, looking at Clayt long and hard all the while. "You don't have a problem with me taking Melody out, do you?"

Grimacing a little, Clayt said, "Do I look like her father?"

"Of course not," Ben said. "It's just that I, that is, everybody, always assumed that the two of you would end up together, what with the crush she had on you all those years. But I was talkin' to Boomer the other day and he happened to mention that Jed Winters told him that Grover Andrews said that Karl Hanson claims that Melody's over you."

Clayt could have done without hearing the whole spiel a second time. Since Ben was his neighbor and there wasn't any polite way to interrupt him, Clayt waited until it was over to say, "I heard that, too."

"Then it's true?" Ben asked.

"She's going out with you tonight, isn't she?"

Ben's mouth slid into a grin. "Yeah, I guess she is. You know, it's kind of funny, but until lately, I never noticed how pretty our very own Melody McCully really is."

"Yeah." To his own ears, Clayt's voice sounded a lot like the last echo of the day. Cramming his hat on his head, he turned on his heel and headed for the door.

He stood at the top of the steps for a few seconds, waiting for his heart rate to return to normal. Feeling more alone than he'd felt in a long, long time, he walked down the stairs and slowly made his way out to the alley where his truck was parked. Six months ago he would have headed for the Crazy Horse. Now he had Haley to consider. Glancing up just in time to see Ben helping Mel into her coat, Clayt climbed into his truck and drove home.

"Hey, Clayt, pour me a cup of that, would you?" Wyatt McCully asked, leaning back in his office chair.

"Me, too," Luke said around the perpetual grin he wore these days.

Sloshing coffee into two more mugs, Clayt had to bite his tongue to keep from asking, When in Sam Hill had they started viewing him as their personal servant?

"What's the matter, Clayt?" Luke asked his brother. "Cat got your tongue?"

Clayt carried all three mugs to Wyatt's old metal desk. Shoving one in Luke's direction and one in Wyatt's, he grasped his own and took a seat. Another time he would have admitted that it was good to have Luke and Wyatt home from their honeymoons. Today his ego was still too sore to admit anything.

"You look like a man who could use a vacation," Luke said. "I highly recommend Cancún."

"The Bahamas were great, too," Wyatt said, yawning and grinning at the same time.

Clayt shook his head. With a ranch to run and his father in Oregon, a vacation was nowhere in the near future. Shaking his head a second time, he said, "For two men who just got back from two of the sunniest spots in the world, you don't look very tanned."

Wyatt grinned again, and Luke said, "Jillian and I didn't get out of the room all that much."

Clayt snorted. "Spare me the details, will ya?"

"Geez, Clayt," Luke declared. "You're acting like a stallion with a sore..."

"Ahh," Clayt said, taking his first sip of coffee. "Now that's the way coffee's supposed to taste. A rich, full brew completely lacking the aftertaste of dirty dishrags."

"You referring to anybody's coffee in particular?" Wyatt asked, opening a file on his desk.

Glancing around the old-fashioned sheriff's office, Clayt said, "Mel's is so thick it's more like paint remover."

With a shrewdness a person rarely noticed with the first look, Wyatt McCully feigned an offhand shrug and said, "You and Mel been sparring again?"

"Is the sky blue again today?" Clayt grumbled. "Her hair might be shorter and she might have treated herself to new clothes. She can even claim she wants everybody to call her *Melody* now, but she's still as ornery and contrary as she's always been." Glancing sheepishly at Wyatt, who happened to be her only brother, he added, "No offense."

Wyatt shared a long look with Luke before holding up his hands. "No offense taken."

"Is there something you want to talk about?" Luke asked.

Clayt glanced from the worry in his brother's gray eyes to the speculation in Wyatt's brown ones. Did he want to talk about it? Hell, no, he didn't want to talk about it. Kissing Mel had been a once-in-a-lifetime aberration, a momentary complete and utter loss of his mind. Mel McCully was simply not the woman for him. He'd been foolish to have considered marrying her. It had been a bad experience, a bad idea. He didn't have to examine the situation with a fine-tooth comb, and he would appreciate it if Luke and Wyatt would drop the subject.

"Is something going on between you and my sister?"

Clayt wasn't sure he hid his guilty expression before Wyatt had noticed, but he was pretty sure the vehemence in the shake of his head came through loud and clear. "Hardly. She just gets under my skin, that's all."

"What did she do now?" Wyatt asked.

"Nothing new." He grimaced a little, because kissing her had been a new experience. Since dredging it up would have been digressing, he said, "You know, the first clear recollection I have of her is the day she started kindergarten. She had her hair in those silly, lopsided pigtails she used to wear. I felt kind of sorry for her, so I asked her if she was scared. She told me to drop dead."

Wyatt chuckled. "Sounds a lot like Haley, doesn't it?"

Clayt was in no frame of mind to see any irony or humor in that particular observation. Deciding it probably wouldn't be wise to start a fistfight with his best friend on his first day back to work following his honeymoon, Clayt continued as if he hadn't heard. "I was in the fourth grade.

Every day for an entire week after that she stuck her tongue out at me whenever she saw me.''

"That was right after our parents drowned, Clayt. Mel was angry back then."

"Yeah?" Clayt grumbled. "Well, she must have still been angry three years later when she kicked me in the shin."

"You have a good memory."

Wyatt McCully wasn't a man to offer empty compliments. It made this one all the more comforting to Clayt's sore ego. This was more like it, he thought, his chest expanding. Yes sirree, it really was good to have Luke and Wyatt back.

"Do you remember that kind of stuff about any other girls?" Wyatt asked, peering at some small print on a form in front of him.

The coffee Clayt had just slurped got stuck halfway down his throat. His face turned red and his throat convulsed. By the time he could talk again, Wyatt was looking at him with the expression that made him a darn good poker player and an even better sheriff.

Getting under Clayt's skin must have been in the McCully blood. When Luke said, "Then you don't have any clear memories of other girls?" Clayt knew it was in the Carson blood, too.

They could needle him and psychoanalyze him all they wanted, but they couldn't make him answer. Wyatt continued as if he had. "Ever ask yourself why?"

Clayt didn't like the direction this conversation had taken. "Look," he said, his voice going ominously low. "I know what you two are thinking, and you can forget it. I tried being nice to that woman. She might as well have been in kindergarten all over again. No sirree, I've had it with Mel—*Melody*—McCully. Haley needs a mother, but

I don't need that kind of grief. So I guess I'll just have to keep looking."

The door opened behind them and a woman's deep, sultry voice drew three pairs of eyes.

"Excuse me." A tall, voluptuous brunette in skintight pants and a stretchy red sweater smiled sweetly. "I seem to be a little lost. Could you all tell me where Pike Street is?"

Clayt found his feet slowly and graced her with his hundred-watt smile. Later he'd razz Luke and Wyatt about the fact that marriage had already made them slow on the take-off, but for now, he made his way toward the door.

Extending his hand, he said, "My name is Clayt Carson. This is Sheriff Wyatt McCully, and my brother, Luke. You're looking for Pike Street? It just so happens I'm going your way."

"Oh, thank you. Thank you so much. I'm Pamela Sue Stanaway, and I will be eternally grateful to you for your kindness."

The woman smiled and wiggled a little, causing Clayt to fear for the seam of her pants. Normally he preferred women who were a little less flashy. Eyeing the fit of Pamela Sue's red sweater, he decided it was high time he became a little more tolerant.

"Right this way, Miss Stanaway," he said, opening the door.

Pamela Sue Stanaway practically batted her eyelashes. "Your advertisement said you boys were shy but willing, but it didn't say you were gentlemen, too."

Clayt shrugged at Luke and Wyatt and offered Pamela Sue his arm. Luke and Wyatt exchanged a worried look. "You're coming to the dinner party Jillian and Lisa are having tomorrow night, aren't you?" Luke called.

"Lisa's counting on you," Wyatt added.

"I'll be there," Clayt answered. "Who knows. I might even bring a friend."

"I do declare, Jillian, this food is delicious."

Jillian Carson cast an apologetic look at Melody before smiling at Pamela Sue Stanaway. "I'm afraid I can't take credit for the delicious meal. Lisa did the cooking and Melody brought dessert. I can't seem to boil water."

Luke snagged his wife's hand and said, "Jillian's expertise tends to run in other areas."

"I do declare," Pamela Sue said in a deep, sultry voice that called to mind magnolia blossoms and long, hoop-skirts, "but you Carsons are a breath of fresh air."

Melody did everything in her power to keep her eyes trained on the food on her plate. Every time she heard that Southern accent, she became more certain she was going to be sick.

Speculation about Clayt and Pamela Sue had been running rampant since yesterday. Most of the Jasper Gents had reacted to Pamela Sue the same way Clayt had. Mouths gaping, eyes bulging, minds boggled.

Isabell Pruitt, the straitlaced, Bible-thumping, self-appointed leader of the Ladies' Aid Society, hadn't wasted any time bringing up the subject earlier that afternoon. The old spinster had come into the diner on the pretense of being thirsty. The glass of iced tea she'd ordered had been nothing more than a cover-up for the real reason she was there. Gossip.

Pounding her bony fist on the table, Isabell had declared, "If I've said it once, I've said it a hundred times. Harlots and women of ill repute, that's who that advertisement will lure to our peaceful town."

"What's a woman of ill repute?" Haley, who had been bussing tables, had asked.

What little chin old Isabell had been born with had nearly

disappeared as she'd fumbled for an answer. "Er, um, they're, well, let's see. They're not the kind of women we want in Jasper Gulch, that's all I can say."

Mel had taken the bus tub Haley had filled and said, "You've talked about Mary Magdalene in Sunday school, haven't you?"

Isabell had nodded as if Melody was doing a fine job of explaining things.

"Mary Magdalene was a woman of ill repute?" Haley asked, looking more like a forlorn little waif than ever with the yellow and purple bruise underneath her right eye. "Miss Opal says we're not supposed to judge other people. We're all supposed to be friends."

Mel had hidden a smile to herself at Isabell's stricken expression. "That's a good point, Haley," Mel had said with a wink. "Let's take these dishes into the kitchen so you can get started."

That had been hours ago. Hours before Melody had actually seen Miss Pamela Sue Stanaway with her own two eyes or heard her with her own two ears. Now that she'd experienced both those things, she was a little less prone to graciousness. It just plain wasn't easy to be gracious while being consumed with jealousy.

"You mean to tell me that little old advertisement you boys placed in the papers produced a double wedding? I do declare that's the most romantic thing I've ever heard."

All eyes turned to Pamela Sue, who was smiling sweetly, although Mel was pretty sure the men in the room weren't actually looking at the other woman's face. Jillian must have noticed the way Haley was staring at Pamela Sue, because she said, "Haley, would you like to help me serve dessert?"

Haley shook her head and stared at the brunette who seemed intent upon touching Clayt at every opportunity. Mel held her breath and tried to catch Haley's attention.

Undeterred, the little girl said, "Are you really a woman of ill repute like Mary Magdalene?"

The dozen people sitting around the big oak table in Luke and Jillian's house gasped. Cletus cleared his throat, Lisa and Jillian exchanged worried glances, and Clayt looked decidedly ill at ease. Pamela Sue Stanaway laughed behind her hand and said, "Gracious, no. Why, I'm just a Southern belle who's looking for a kind and gentle man."

Haley rolled her eyes and Melody almost did.

Lisa served Melody's warm apple pie. Earlier Mel's mouth had been watering for a taste of sweet apples and cinnamon, but she had lost her appetite. She placed one hand on her stomach, the other to her lips. She was coming down with something, she was sure of it.

Melody's stomach was still roiling two nights later. She was ill, all right. But she had love sickness, not the flu.

"Here," DoraLee said, plunking a shot glass and a bottle of whiskey in front of her at the bar. "Drink this. Maybe it'll put a little color back in your cheeks."

Keeping her eyes trained on her friend and not on the big mirror behind the bar, Melody took the small glass in her hand and knocked back the shot. Gasping for air, she slammed the glass down on the bar and rasped, "Fill her up, DoraLee."

"Oh, sugar," DoraLee whispered. "Are you sure?"

Sultry laughter carried to Melody's ears over the Willie Nelson tune playing from the jukebox in one corner and the poker game being played earnestly in another. Of their own volition, Melody's eyes strayed to the mirror just as Pamela Sue Stanaway wiggled her bottom onto Clayt's lap in the back of the room.

"Believe me, DoraLee. I'm sure."

The second shot burned a bigger hole in her stomach than the first one had, but neither of them took away the dull ache deep inside. "Hurry, DoraLee," Melody whispered. "Tell me something good, something happy."

Patting her coiffed, bleached blond hair, DoraLee sidled closer and whispered, "Well, Boomer and I weren't going to tell anybody just yet, so I'd appreciate it if you wouldn't mention this to another soul. Boomer asked me to marry him last night. And I accepted."

Melody slid off her stool and ran around to the other side of the bar where she hugged her dear friend and whispered her congratulations. "Oh, DoraLee, that is good news. You deserve happiness more than anybody I know."

Smiling a little sadly, DoraLee said, "So do you, sugar. So do you."

Melody blinked her eyes and clamped her lips together to ward off a sob. She reminded herself that she still had her diner, and she still had her pride. Those things seemed like small consolation for her breaking heart. Telling herself it was her own fault didn't help. Calling herself a fool for harboring such silly, unrealistic fantasies and dreams of romance and true love didn't, either.

While DoraLee filled three steins from the tap behind the bar, Melody slipped into the back room. Staying in the shadows, she glanced at Clayt just as Pamela Sue planted a great big kiss on his lean cheek. Apparently Cletus was right, that it did surprise the patooty out of most men, because Clayt looked as if he was seeing stars.

Mel managed to blink back all but one tear and took a shuddering breath. It was just like watching Victoria in action all over again. To her credit, Pamela Sue didn't seem mean-spirited. That wasn't much consolation, either.

Feeling strangely cold despite the whiskey that had burned a path from her throat all the way to the pit of her stomach, Melody slipped out the back door. Hurrying through the gloom of the cloudy autumn night, she ran around the block, not stopping until she'd climbed the steps and was safe inside her apartment.

Not bothering to turn on a light, she sank to her knees in the middle of her living room rug. She squeezed her eyes shut, but she couldn't seem to get the image of Clayt and Pamela Sue out of her mind.

Ten years ago she'd stood by and watched Clayt pursue Victoria. She couldn't go through that again. She couldn't go to his wedding a second time and wish him well. She couldn't love him from afar when he came into the diner for supper three times a week. She couldn't spend her last waking thoughts thinking about him, knowing that he was crawling into bed with someone else.

Rocking back and forth, Melody buried her face in her hands and tried to think of what other choice she had.

Chapter Five

At three o'clock the following afternoon, Melody was no closer to finding a solution to her dilemma than she'd ever been. It had been a madhouse at the diner all day, but at least the scalloped potatoes and ham she served every other Thursday was ready to be baked. Hoisting the dish into the fifty-year-old oven, she set the temperature and closed the door.

She enjoyed cooking and found a certain degree of satisfaction in knowing she was good at what she did. Every night had its own special. Mesquite steak on Monday, meat loaf on Tuesday, rib eye and baby potatoes on Wednesday, scalloped potatoes with baked ham on alternating Thursdays, and three-siren chili on Friday. A person could get a cheeseburger, fried chicken or a sandwich any day of the week, and liver and onions the first Tuesday of every month. Mertyl Gentry asked for a bowl of homemade oatmeal every morning, while Cletus ordered up steak and eggs. The place was more famous for its homemade pies than its vegetables, but the main course—morning, noon and night—was always the same: gossip. And today had been no exception.

Speculation was running rampant that there was going to be another wedding in Jasper Gulch, and folks weren't referring to Boomer and DoraLee. Melody's heart was going to be broken again, and there didn't seem to be a thing she could do about it. She'd had her chance. And she'd missed it. All because of her stupid pride and her foolish dreams.

Her deep sigh filled the empty kitchen just as the bell over the door jingled in the dining room. It looked as if her new dishwasher was a few minutes early. "Come on back, Haley," she called.

The door opened, but it was Louetta Graham who poked her head inside, not Haley. Louetta was only a few years older than Melody, but she wore her hair in a severe bun and was so painfully shy she seemed old beyond her years.

"Hi, Louetta," Melody said warmly. "What's the matter? Can't you get enough of this place during your weekly Tuesday lunches with your mother?"

Color stained Louetta's pale cheeks. Louetta Graham was always blushing about something. Tucking a piece of mousy brown hair into her bun, she said, "Actually, I'm here about the Help Wanted sign I saw in the window."

"You want to be a waitress?" Melody asked incredulously.

Louetta's eyes dropped to the toes of her sensible shoes. "Yes, I'd at least like the chance to try. I've been working for Isabell in the library for years, but now that Mother and Isabell aren't speaking, it's gotten terribly awkward. I've been wanting to make some changes in my life for some time, and I saw your ad, and I just thought this might be the perfect opportunity. Of course, I'll understand if you want someone with more experience..."

"If you can pour coffee, the job's yours."

Louetta's double take was almost comical. "Do you mean you're hiring me just like that?"

Melody smiled for the first time all day. "I need a waitress. You need a job. When can you start?"

Louetta blushed all over again, causing Melody to wonder what the Jasper Gents were going to say about their new waitress. The bell over the front door jingled a second time. "That'll be the dishwasher," she explained to Louetta. "Come on back," she called to Haley.

"It's me, Mel. Can I talk to you a minute?"

Once again Melody recognized the deep timbre of Clayt's voice. Once again she recognized what it did to her. Hope sprang anew as she slowly turned around.

Clayt wore his dark brown Stetson low on his forehead. He hadn't shaved in a day or two, but his blue cotton shirt looked clean and his boots looked polished.

"Are you going somewhere?" she asked.

Clayt Carson wasn't a man prone to smiles. It only made the one he slanted her way right then all the more noteworthy. "Yeah, that's what I wanted to talk to you about. I thought I'd take Haley shopping."

A force bigger than her had her walking closer. "*You're* going shopping?"

"Pamela Sue's coming with us."

Melody's feet froze to the floor. She thought she did a pretty good job of hiding her disappointment. She only hoped Clayt didn't notice it in her voice when she said, "I'm kind of busy right now. What did you want to talk to me about?"

The noise Louetta made behind her seemed to bring Clayt to his senses. With a tug at the brim of his hat he nodded at Louetta before turning his attention back to Melody. "I just wanted you to know that Haley can't work this afternoon."

"That's fine, Clayt. Whatever."

He looked at her strangely for a moment, causing her to wonder what he was thinking. Before she could figure it out, he said, "Oh, by the way, Haley says she's hungry. Pamela Sue thought it might be nice if we got something to eat before heading into Pierre."

The thought of waiting on the three of them as if they were a family made Melody's heart ache around the edges and her throat constrict. Swallowing the fist-sized lump that had formed around her voice box, she said, "There won't be a full menu to choose from this time of the day."

He nodded. "No problem. Haley and I will probably order a sandwich, and Pamela Sue eats like a bird, anyway."

He smiled again, pulled at the brim of his hat and strode away. Louetta joined Melody in the doorway. Peering through a small crack, they watched Clayt stroll to the booth where Haley and Pamela Sue were waiting.

"No matter what Clayt says," Louetta whispered, "that woman didn't fill out those jeans and that sweater by eating like a bird."

Melody was so surprised to hear Louetta say anything of the kind she could only stare. With a telltale blush tingeing her cheeks, Louetta tied an apron over her starched skirt and reached for Melody's pad and pencil. "In answer to your earlier question, I can start right away."

Gazing after Louetta, who was walking stiffly into the dining room, Melody could hardly believe her eyes or her ears. Louetta Graham had always been as quiet as a mouse and just as shy. Obviously there was more to her than met the eye.

The sultry lilt of Pamela Sue's laughter drew Melody's attention. It didn't take much insight to figure out what Clayt saw in that particular Southern belle. Not that there was anything wrong with her. Aside from the fact that she wore her clothes two sizes too small, she was very nice.

Melody could be nice when she wanted to be. Pamela Sue was also very stacked. And Melody couldn't compete with that no matter how hard she tried.

Aside from praying for a miracle, it looked as if the situation was completely hopeless. And so was she.

Melody was sitting in her normal pew in church the following Sunday, Cletus on one side of her, Wyatt and Lisa on the other. She supposed she was in the right place to pray for a miracle. She just wasn't so sure praying for larger breasts was an honorable and justifiable request.

Deciding it might be better to ask for insight and strength, she folded her hands. She was so in tune with her prayers she barely noticed the folks of Jasper Gulch who were taking their seats. She was vaguely aware that Clayt and Haley had slid into a pew on the other side of the aisle, where the Carsons had been sitting for as long as she could remember. Closing her eyes, she concentrated all the harder.

A murmur went through the church, but it wasn't until after she'd said, "Amen," that she understood what had instigated it. Clayt was sitting in his usual spot all right. And perched right next to him was a dainty little princess formerly known as Haley Carson.

Good Lord, what did they do to her? That poor little girl was dressed in pink from head to toe. There were ribbons in her hair, ruffles on her sleeves and lace on her socks. She reminded Melody of a faithful old dog who'd been forced to bear the indignities of wearing doll clothes. Head hung low, eyes downcast, Haley looked as if she wanted to disappear. She glanced back at Melody only once, and the look in those eyes that usually were full of mischief almost broke Melody's heart.

The organ music changed and the congregation stood. Melody forced her eyes straight ahead, but when the service was over, she couldn't remember a single word Reverend Jones had uttered. She was still thinking about Haley when she trudged back up the stairs to her place a short time later. Haley needed a woman who understood her. And Melody needed Clayt to love her. It was a mess, and it still seemed as hopeless as ever.

The day stretched before her, bleak and lonely. She knew she was always welcome at her grandfather's house, but she wasn't up to listening to any more of his advice concerning her and Clayt. Wyatt and Lisa had told her to stop by anytime. But they were newlyweds and deserved a little privacy.

She ran the zipper down the back of another of her new dresses as she strode through her tiny living room. Upon reaching her bedroom, she tossed the dress on the bed and kicked off her shoes. Catching her reflection in the antique mirror that had belonged to her mother, she stopped and slowly turned. At five foot three, her body was lean and lithe and, she supposed, attractive in its own way. She'd faced the fact that she would never fill out a sweater the way Pamela Sue did. Until lately, she hadn't wanted to. She was comfortable with her body. She didn't need bras with wide straps or underwires or special support. With the right shirt, she didn't need a bra at all. Feeling more like her old self, she reached behind her and unfastened her bra. It landed on the bed next to her dress.

Ten years ago she hadn't been able to compete with Victoria's cool sophistication and classic beauty. Now it seemed she couldn't compete with a lilting Southern accent and a thirty-eight-D bra size. *What is, is,* she whispered to herself. Feeling free and the tiniest bit naughty, she tugged on a pair of her softest jeans and took a thick, cotton shirt off a hanger. Since she was opting for comfort, she scrubbed her face, finger combed her hair and pulled on her favorite cowboy boots. She was in the process of tucking in her shirt when a knock sounded on the door.

She'd barely turned the knob before Clayt pushed through, his expression taut with worry. "Have you seen Haley?"

"Not since church. Why?"

He took off his hat and ran a hand through his hair. "She ran away again."

Melody closed the door and tried to take in what Clayt had said. "When did you see her last?"

"Right after we got home from church. She said she wanted to go say hello to her horse. When I called her in for dinner, she was gone."

Melody stopped pacing and slowly turned. Eyeing Clayt, she said, "She didn't change her clothes?"

He shook his head once, his eyes narrowing. "What does that have to do with anything?"

"If she's still wearing that dress, she hasn't gone far."

Clayt released all the air in his lungs through pursed lips. "Then it's possible those ruffles and bows were a little too much?"

It was all Melody could do not to roll her eyes. "Maybe just a smidge. I'm amazed you ever talked her into wearing all that prissy stuff in the first place."

Clayt heaved another sigh and shook his head. "It was Pamela Sue's idea. She thought Haley might fit in with the other little girls in her class if she dressed more femininely. I thought she might have been on to something, and maybe a few subtle changes would help Haley. Just look at you."

Feeling as if her wits were being rejuvenated one by one, Melody started to smile. Why, that had almost sounded like a compliment. She would have liked to ask Clayt to elaborate, but he'd started pacing, talking as he went.

"I'm afraid Pamela Sue got carried away. She's just so sweet and nice and kind and well, Southern, and she was having so much fun that Haley and I couldn't bring ourselves to hurt her feelings. She's just so sweet. And kind. And sweet.''

All right, already. Melody got the picture. He could stop using the word *sweet* anytime. Trying not to get huffy, she said, "Did Haley take her horse?"

Clayt shook his head. "Her filly isn't tame enough to ride, but her bike's gone. I wouldn't be so worried if I thought she was on foot." He turned slowly. "Why? Do you think you know where she might be?"

One place came to mind. Nodding, Melody said, "We need to stop at your house first."

Clayt was already waiting for her at the door.

Fifteen minutes later he parked his truck in a bumpy lane at the base of a rickety old bridge that spanned Sugar Creek. A little farther upstream was a wide spot that was deep enough for swimming. After a heavy rain the current underneath the bridge could be treacherous, but today the water was only a few feet deep and was more like a babbling brook than a raging river.

"You think she's around here?" Clayt asked, throwing the gearshift lever into Park.

Glancing around, Melody nodded. The tips of the leaves on the old oak trees on the other side of the creek were beginning to turn brown, but only a few had fallen. The sun was shining; the air was a mixture of summer and autumn, the creek somehow caught in between.

"What makes you think she's here?" Clayt asked.

Pulling up on her door handle, Melody said, "Just the other day she told me she liked to come here. I'm not surprised. It's where I always came when I wanted to be alone."

"I didn't know that."

"Just think, Clayt, there might even be one or two other things you don't know about me."

Melody had turned in her seat, her feet dangling out the door. Glancing over her shoulder, she found Clayt looking at her exactly the way he'd looked at her a hundred other times when she'd said something sarcastic. Shoot. She hadn't meant to let that slip, and she certainly hadn't intended to sound so confounded nasty. No wonder Clayt had never accused *her* of being *sweet*.

"Come on," she said, sliding to the ground. "Unless I miss my guess, Haley saw us drive up."

She led the way to a trail that looked freshly trampled. Veering around some scrub brush, they came to a dilapidated fort that had been built some twenty-odd years ago by a group of local boys who'd long since grown up. A shiny purple bike was parked nearby.

Scooping up a pink ribbon Haley had been wearing in her hair earlier, Clayt practically ran the rest of the way. He hadn't been expecting the door to be bolted from inside, and had to practically peel himself off the door. "Haley," he called, wiggling the handle. "Open up."

Laying a hand on his arm, Melody gestured for him to follow her lead. "It's a nice day for a stroll, isn't it Clayt?"

"Yeah, real nice, Mel, er, Melody, real nice, indeed," he said, making her glad he was a rancher and would never have to rely on his acting skills to earn a living.

Gesturing with her head, Melody said, "Why don't you go on down by the water and skip a few stones."

"All right," he said, hitching his fingers through his belt loops. "I think I'll do that."

When he was out of sight, Melody said, "It's okay, Haley. You can come out now."

The heavy silence didn't fool Melody. Trying a different tack, she crossed her arms and started to whistle. As if she had all the time in the world, she said, "Hey, I've got a joke for you. Pete and re-Pete are in a boat. Pete falls out. Who's left?''

More silence.

"Come on, Haley. What do you say?''

"I say that's a stupid joke.''

Melody placed her hand over her heart. "It's one of my favorites. Come on, who's left?''

"Re-Pete's left,'' Haley said grudgingly.

"Who?''

"Re-Pete.''

Melody grinned. "Pete and re-Pete are in a boat...''

"I'm still not coming out.''

"Do you think I care what you look like, Haley?''

Other than a few early leaves twirling down from the branches overhead and the water trickling over stones in the creek, the afternoon remained perfectly quiet.

"I brought you a change of clothes,'' Melody cajoled.

"You did?''

"Yup.''

"What did ya bring me?''

"Blue jeans and your red shirt with the sunflower on it.''

Melody heard the girl's sigh all the way from here. "You have to help me,'' she whispered.

"Help you with what?'' Melody asked.

"You can't let Clayton marry that woman.''

It was Melody's turn to sigh. Leaving the clothes on the ground, she retraced her steps over the path, thereby giving Haley a little space in which to restore her dignity.

A stone plopped into the creek twenty-five feet away. Following the curve in the trail, Melody strolled down to the creek bank where Clayt was sitting on a fallen log. "Is she coming out?'' he asked, turning a stone over and over in his hand.

"I think so.''

"Did she sound all right to you?''

"She was a little standoffish, but I'm pretty sure the only thing injured is her pride."

Clayt propped one boot on a nearby rock and rotated a kink out of his shoulders. "I don't know how you manage it, but you can get my daughter to do things no one else can."

She only shrugged. Mel McCully never had been one to brag. Raising her arms for balance, she stepped onto the creek bank and slid down the smooth surface. It was funny. He'd seen her perform similar maneuvers a hundred times, yet he'd never really noticed how lithe and graceful she was. Except for her hair, she looked more like the old Mel today. Her jeans were faded, her face was clean scrubbed, her lips a natural shade of pink. Those full, pink, wet lips.

He'd lost count of how many times he'd caught himself staring at her mouth. He couldn't seem to get the memory of how her lips had felt against his out of his mind. He couldn't forget the way she'd felt in his arms or how her sigh had sounded in his ears, either.

Once again desire uncurled low in his abdomen. Shifting his position on the fallen log, he knew of one surefire way to eliminate the sensation. If he could get Mel talking she would invariably make him angry, and that would be that.

Tucking a piece of dry prairie grass between his teeth, he said, "Wyatt thinks the reason you're so good with Haley is because she's a lot like you."

She hopped onto a flat rock that was sticking out of the water before replying. "That probably went over like a brick balloon, huh?"

Clayt knew all he had to do was agree and Mel would get angry once and for all. But she raised her face to the sky as if she wanted to embrace the breeze, and suddenly his throat felt thick, and he found himself saying, "Maybe it means she'll grow up strong and independent and graceful. Like you."

Balancing on the next stone, she glanced over her shoulder, straight into his eyes. "Are you flirting with me, Clayt?"

He jerked so fast his boot slid to the ground. If she had to ask, he was rustier than he thought. "Hell no," he said, jumping to his feet. "Where in the world did you get that idea?"

Gauging the distance between the stone she was standing on and the one she wanted to jump to next, Melody sighed. Of course Clayt wasn't flirting with her. Just look at her. She wasn't wearing a scrap of makeup, and she probably looked about fourteen in her faded jeans and thick cotton shirt. Two compliments from Clayt Carson in one day had to be some kind of record, but it didn't mean he was attracted to her.

Curious, she said, "You really think the subtle changes I've made in my appearance have helped?"

One moment her knees and elbows were bent, the next she was airborne. Her right boot scudded as it came into contact with the smooth stone. Balancing on one foot, she glanced back at Clayt.

He stood very still, watching her. For an instant the breeze died away. Only the water trickling over the rocks covered the erratic thud of her heart. She wished she was closer, so she could see if she was imagining the heat in his eyes. For a moment she felt suspended in time. And then her foot began to slip; her arms flailed. From the corner of her eye she saw Clayt jump onto the first stone. And then she was falling backward.

The cold water was a shock to her senses, the hard bottom of the creek a surprise to something else entirely.

"Mel, are you all right?"

She was sitting on the bottom of the creek bed, her knees and shoulders sticking out of the chilly water. She glanced up at Clayt, who was straddling two of the rocks closest to her.

Sighing, she said, "Talk about injured pride."

His smile reached down inside her, but any unusual heat in his eyes must have been a figment of her imagination, because his eyes were crinkled at the corners and were glimmering with a friendly light and nothing more. When he offered her his hand, she took it, letting him pull her to her feet. Water sluiced down her body, plastering her jeans to her thighs, filling her most comfortable cowboy boots.

Pushing her hair out of her face, she tried to tug her hand out of Clayt's. His grip remained firm, his palm warm.

She tipped her head back, all ready to grant him a sheepish smile of gratitude, but one look at his face, and her own smile trailed away. He was looking at her, staring at her. But not at her face. She glanced down, and understanding dawned. Dry, her white shirt was as thick and pristine as a nun's habit. Wet, it was as transparent as onion skin. And she wasn't wearing a bra.

Her nipples were puckered from the cold, the areolae pale, pale pink. Her breasts rose and fell with every breath she took, and quivered slightly when she shivered.

She swallowed, then tugged again on Clayt's hand. He released her, finally, and slowly brought his eyes to hers. She should have been freezing, but the expression on his face warmed her as she'd never been warmed before. His eyes had darkened to the color of smoke, his lips were pressed together, a muscle working in one lean cheek. It was the kind of look only a man could give a woman, the kind of look that made her feel beautiful in a way that transcended eye color and skin.

Clayt couldn't breathe or move or think. He knew what was coming over him. But he didn't know how to stop it. Telling himself that this was Mel McCully didn't help, because Mel McCully had never looked like this before. Wet, her hair appeared darker, exotic almost. Moisture clung to her cheek, and her eyes were wide and blue and dewy. This was the same Mel he'd grown up with, yet there was something different about her, something feminine and womanly and earthy. It wasn't just the fact that he could see her breasts. He'd seen breasts before. Although he'd never seen hers. And he'd never toyed with the idea of joining her in the water, of unbuttoning her blouse and discovering for himself how that cream-colored flesh would feel in the palm of his hand.

This entire day seemed like a coincidence of miraculous proportions. He'd been harboring some incredibly stimulating fantasies, and coincidence or not, any man would react this way, even if the woman *was* his best friend's kid sister. Only Mel, he gulped, Melody, wasn't all skinny legs and knobby knees anymore. Dripping wet, there was a flare to her hips, and he swore she had the most graceful neck he'd ever seen. And lower. He swallowed, because try as he might, he couldn't think of a word to describe what he was staring at lower. However, he knew exactly how to describe what *looking* was doing to his body.

"Melody," Haley called, sliding down the bank. "What happened? Why are you all wet?"

Clayt came to his senses at the same time Haley scampered onto the first stepping-stone. Dressed in blue jeans and a red shirt, she looked more like her old self, while he felt less like himself than he ever had in his life.

"Wow, Melody," Haley called, coming to a stop near her father, "I can see your boobies."

Melody pulled her shirt away from her body. The instant she let it go, it conformed to her skin, becoming transparent all over again. Dragging her eyes from Clayt's, she took a deep breath. Turning her back on father and daughter, she trudged through the knee-deep water, not stopping until she was on the bank on the other side.

"What's wrong with her?" she heard Haley say behind her.

"I think she's embarrassed," Clayt answered.

"Why should she be embarrassed? You and I are the only people who saw her boobies. The whole town saw me in church today."

"Come on, Haley," Clayt said, his voice suspiciously husky. "Let's go home."

"Is Melody coming, too?"

"Yeah, kiddo, Melody's definitely coming, too."

Mel settled onto her couch, where she tried to concentrate on the rodeo on television. She crossed her legs and jiggled one foot. She lasted about as long as the rodeo rider lasted on the bull's back, she and the cowboy springing to their feet at the same time. If she'd seen one cowboy being bucked off a high-kicking, knee-jerking, head-swinging, body-twisting bull once, she'd seen it a thousand times.

While the announcer shouted over the crowd in the background, Melody glanced around her own living room. The carpet could have used another once-over with a vacuum cleaner, and she supposed she could have tackled the closet. But she was too fidgety for either of those things. It was after seven o'clock. At this rate she was going to wear out two pairs of boots in one day.

Clayt had been adamant about taking her back to his place after that little episode at the creek earlier that afternoon. She'd been equally adamant about coming straight back here. The man could bully most people into doing what he wanted. But he should have learned by now that he couldn't bully her.

He hadn't been able to see any reason why she shouldn't simply do as he asked and don one of his dry shirts so they could talk about what had happened and put it in perspective. By perspective, Melody knew he meant he wanted things to go back to the way they used to be. Since the last thing Melody wanted was for things to go back to the way they used to be, she'd held her ground.

She knew she'd probably been a sight, huddled next to the door in his truck where she'd covered herself with Haley's ruffled pink dress while Haley chattered and Clayt drove her home, but she didn't care. Her future happiness was at stake, and that was more important than how she looked.

By the time Clayt had dropped her off in the back alley that led to her apartment, he'd been thoroughly exasperated and completely convinced that her behavior was due to intense embarrassment. He was wrong. Strangely, she wasn't embarrassed. She felt empowered by the expression she'd seen on his face that afternoon, and the slight change in the fit of his jeans. She wouldn't go back to his house with him because they would probably argue and he would convince himself that what he'd felt had been the result of hormones and she was really the same old Mel she'd always been. She wasn't about to let that happen.

For years she'd been yearning to have Clayt fall in love with her. She'd always assumed it would be like the little ditty she used to recite when she was a child: "First comes love, then comes marriage, then comes Clayt pushing a baby carriage."

But then she'd fallen in the creek, and he'd seen her wet and womanly, and all of a sudden she'd realized she'd been going about this all wrong. Love hadn't come first with Clayt. Desire had.

She was almost positive he wasn't going to rest easy until he'd convinced himself that he'd imagined his earlier reaction to her, or had at least dismissed it as a silly aberration that would never happen again. The longer he waited to come over, the more nervous she became.

She almost jumped out of her skin when the knock finally sounded on her door. Taking a moment to smooth her hands down her softly gathered skirt and inhale a calming breath, she strode to the door.

Clayt's fist was raised to knock a second time when Mel opened the door. He gave her a curt nod on his way inside. "Look, Mel, I know you're embarrassed about what happened today, but I..."

"I'm not embarrassed, Clayt. And I'm glad you stopped by. And really, I wish you'd call me Melody."

He snapped his mouth shut, but she was already twirling toward the kitchen so she didn't see. "I made coffee. Would you like a cup?"

She disappeared into the next room before he could answer, although now that he thought about it, he might have nodded. She'd made coffee? What the hell was going on? She was acting as if she'd been expecting him.

He almost followed her into the kitchen, but stopped in the doorway at the last minute. The room was barely large enough for one person, and he didn't think it would be wise to get caught in such close quarters with Mel—or Melody or whatever the hell he was supposed to call her now—when his hormones were still a little out of control.

Watching as she reached to a shelf for two mugs, he realized that she really didn't look all that embarrassed. While she talked about the rodeo she'd been watching on television, he told himself there was nothing unusual about the soft white blouse with the scooped neckline she was wearing. And he'd seen a lot of the local women dressed in similar, flowered skirts since Lisa had opened her clothing store on Main Street. Surely it was the three-inch heels on Mel's brown cowboy boots that made her appear as pliant and winsome as a willow switch.

Melody could practically see the battles taking place behind Clayt's eyes. His face, square and handsome and deeply tanned, bore the telltale signs of confusion. It was all she could do not to reach up on tiptoe and whisper a kiss along the furrow in his brow.

Handing him a mug of steaming coffee, she granted him a smile that earned her a long, speculative look. Feeling giddy and the tiniest bit bold, she said, "I've been thinking a lot about Haley since this afternoon."

"You have?"

She nodded. "I don't like the fact that she ran away again today."

"That has me worried, too. Although I'm pretty sure she only did it because she was ashamed of being dressed like Pollyanna when everyone knows she's a blue jeans and T-shirt little girl."

"Yes," Mel said, striding just close enough so that Clayt would get a whiff of her perfume. "But the fact that she succumbed at all proves that she's a lot more vulnerable than she lets on."

"I'm afraid that's true." He breathed deeply, a dazed look settling over his features. Following her to the sofa, he sat down. "I know I'm in over my head where that little girl is concerned, and I doubt I'll ever win any father-of-the-year awards. But I love that kid more than I've ever loved anyone in my life. And while I can't take all the credit for her wit and intelligence, I'm not going to take all the blame for her insecurities, either. Victoria's desertion has been hard on Haley. It's the main reason I've been searching for a mother for her."

"I understand, Clayt."

"You do?"

She made a humming sound that meant yes. "That's what I wanted to talk to you about."

"It is?"

"Yes, but before I go any further, there's something I want to know."

"What?"

Placing her coffee cup on the low table, she said, "How do you feel about Pamela Sue? That is, do you think you're falling in love with her?"

Clayt blew on his steaming coffee. "She's sweet, she really is. And Lord, that body..."

Great, Melody thought, *here we go again.*

"She tries," he said, "and she seems like a good person. She's just so sweet."

The change in the tone of his voice changed everything. Suddenly *sweet* no longer grated on Melody's nerves.

"It's a little like that first bite of fudge," he said, lowering his cup of coffee to one knee. "At first it's like heaven, but after a while a man starts to crave something with more substance, something solid, something he can sink his teeth into."

Melody's breath caught in her throat as his gaze dropped from her eyes, to her lips, to her neck and lower. It took everything she had to keep from throwing herself into his arms then and there. Holding on to her composure, she placed her hand on his arm and said, "In that case, there's something I want you to know."

Like a man who had no idea he was about to step directly into the eye of a storm, he said, "Oh really? What?"

"I've changed my mind. About marrying you."

Clayt stared into Mel's wide blue eyes, speechless. His heart rate sped up, pounding in his ears. He almost asked her to repeat herself. For a second there he thought he'd heard her say she'd marry him. Surely, he'd heard wrong.

"Clayt?"

The butterfly touch of her fingertips sent a different rhythm through his body. He found himself staring at the small, chapped hand on his arm.

"Are you all right?" she asked.

"Did you say you'll marry me?"

Her eyes looked huge and deep as she nodded.

I'll be damned, he thought to himself. *I must have missed the six o'clock news, because I didn't know that all the other men had fallen off the face of the earth.*

He hadn't realized he'd spoken out loud until Mel bristled. "Do you want me to marry you or don't you?"

His mind cleared and his heart rate returned to normal. That was exactly the tone of voice he'd expected Mel to use. Placing his coffee next to hers, he jumped to his feet and let loose a yowling ye-ha. Rocking back on his heels, he beamed down at her. "Me and little Mel McCully. Who would have believed it."

Melody rose to her feet more slowly. She knew better than to be disappointed because he didn't sound more enthused. But she couldn't help the tiny pinprick she felt in her heart.

"When?" he asked.

"The sooner the better," she answered without meeting his eyes. *Before she lost her nerve.*

"I'll make an appointment for Tuesday with the justice of the peace in Murdo. We can drive over right after you finish with the lunch rush. I'll bet the judge could say 'I now pronounce you husband and wife' fast enough to have you back in the diner for the supper crowd and me back before Haley gets out of school."

"The justice of the peace?" she asked.

"The sooner we get married and settled the better it will be for Haley."

"When will you tell her?" Melody asked.

"It would save a lot of time and trouble if we waited until after the fact. Haley will be surprised, but she thinks the world of you. My folks aren't around, anyway, and yours have been gone for a long time."

She turned away, the dream she'd harbored all these years of wearing her mother's wedding gown slowly fading away.

"Will Tuesday work out for you?" he asked.

Tuesday was two days away. That meant there would be no bridal shower, no engagement party, no whispered words of love and undying devotion. No lace, no preacher, no guests. No romance. "Tuesday sounds fine, Clayt."

"Good. Then it's settled."

Mel tried not to grimace. Casting Clayt a semblance of a smile, she saw him to the door. There was an awkward moment when he turned around to face her. As if he didn't know whether to shake her hand or seal the deal with a kiss, he gave her a peck on the cheek before turning on his heel and ambling toward the stairs.

"You really are being a good sport about this," he said over his shoulder as if he'd asked her to throw a steak on the grill in the middle of the afternoon.

That was her, she thought, listening to his footsteps on the stairs. A good sport to the end.

Chapter Six

"Please join your right hands."

The seventy-year-old justice of the peace looked expectantly at Melody over the top of his reading glasses. Too bad she couldn't drag her eyes any farther than the old light fixture on the wall directly behind his right shoulder. She supposed there was nothing wrong with the courthouse in Murdo. It looked like a hundred other courthouses in a hundred other small towns throughout the West. It just wasn't where she'd planned to utter the most important words of her life, that's all.

She'd been dreaming of marrying Clayt for as long as she could remember, but in her dreams she'd been wearing her mother's gown, candles flickered and the air was heavy with the scent of carnations and mums. Today there were no candles, no flowers, no long white dress. The old light fixtures did little to detract from the gloominess of the brown paneling. This should have been the happiest day of her life, yet she felt as if she were renewing her driver's license.

The justice of the peace cleared his throat, but it was the sound of Clayt's voice as he called her name that drew her gaze. His face was clean shaven, his hair freshly cut. He was wearing his best suit, and although the inherent determination in the set of his chin was the essence of the man, himself, the tender, almost wistful look of entreaty in his eyes was something she'd rarely seen.

She knew he'd always been at his best when he was on the edge, when beef prices were horrid and the weather was worse. His parents' extended stay in Oregon had left him in charge of the ranch, following the worst drought in more than twenty years. Haley's arrival on his doorstep was an even bigger responsibility. The deep groove in one cheek and the new lines beside his eyes were testimony to the weight he now carried single-handedly.

Melody wanted romance. Heaven help her, she wanted love. In that instant she realized that although Clayt wasn't offering her either of those things, he was offering her his hand, and the opportunity to be a part of his life. All she could do was take it and hope that she could lure him into love.

"Is everything all right?" he asked quietly.

She nodded and slowly placed her hand in his. The stoop-shouldered justice of the peace read from his frayed book, while a plump woman with blue hair and trifocals sniffled into a lace handkerchief. Melody answered when appropriate and repeated the proper phrases when it was her turn. She supposed she should have paid closer attention to the words being spoken, but the words themselves didn't matter any more than the setting did. What mattered was the fact that she was finally going to marry the man she loved.

"With the power vested in me by the state of South Dakota, I now pronounce you husband and wife."

She looked up at Clayt. And he looked at her. Amazed

and slightly shaken by the simplicity and profoundness of that statement, she tilted her head to one side. Offering him a tremulous smile, she said, "Aren't you going to kiss your bride?"

Keeping her features deceptively composed, she lifted her face for his kiss. When the quick peck came, she was ready. Going up on tiptoe, she took his face between her hands and whispered, "You can do better than that."

For the first time in her life, she instigated a deep and passionate kiss. Clayt froze for an instant, but it didn't take him long to recover. He made a husky, lusty sound in the back of his throat, and then his arms were winding around her back and he was drawing her against him, his mouth working over hers all the while.

Her knees became weak and her eyelids grew heavy. Okay, she thought to herself, reveling in the power of his embrace. Maybe he didn't love her, but he wanted her. Surely marriages had been built on a lot less.

Somewhere far away the justice of the peace cleared his throat. When their kiss finally broke, Melody smiled at her husband. For now, at least, she would be satisfied with his desire. Before long she intended to draw that desire as taut as one of the Anderson brothers' guitar strings, then gently strum it into love.

"Look at those clouds," Clayt said as his truck crested a hill on Highway 83 on the way back to Jasper Gulch.

"If Granddad was here," Melody said over the country-western song playing on the radio, "he'd say those gray clouds were claiming the sky."

Clayt glanced at Mel's profile. "What do you think Cletus is going to say about us?"

She pretended to snap one suspender. "He's taking all the credit for bringing Luke and Jillian, and Wyatt and Lisa, together. He'll probably take the credit for this, too."

Her voice strummed over his senses, sultry and deep. Since when had Mel become so glowing and warm and—well—so sensual? And since when had he reacted so strongly to the sound of her voice and the scent of her perfume?

Since she'd practically kissed his socks off an hour ago, that's when.

She'd changed out of her peach-colored dress, but her hair was still twisted in some intricate knot on her head, and there were faint traces of makeup on her eyelids and on her cheeks and lips. She looked downright pretty. Before he could tell her so, she met his gaze and smiled. For some strange reason, he felt like smiling, too. It *was* strange. He'd known Mel all her life. She already knew the story of how his great-great-grandfather, Jasper Carson, had founded the town with a little gold he'd found in the Black Hills in his pocket and a widow he'd won in a poker game at his side. They both knew that the history of South Dakota read like an adventure story riddled with tales of daring fur traders and fierce battles with Indians and stampedes for gold. Folks out here always said the true heroes were the farmers and ranchers who'd clung to their land through droughts, locust plagues, blizzards, bottomed-out beef prices and the shortage of women.

There *had* been a shortage of women in Jasper Gulch. There still was. Yet Mel had been here all along, opening her diner no matter what the weather, serving a hot meal with a joke or a smile. Never once in all those years had he had this much trouble keeping his truck between the lines and his hormones under control.

He gripped the steering wheel, a muscle working in his jaw. The butterfly touch of Mel's fingertips sent a different rhythm through his body. His gaze did a slow climb from her hand to the softness in her gaze.

"Is something wrong?" she asked.

He glanced back at the road. "I was just wishing that you didn't have to be back at the diner so I could have taken you out for a proper wedding dinner."

"I appreciate that, Clayt, but I can't close the diner without making everyone in town suspicious. And we both agreed that Haley should be the first to know."

"Then this arrangement is really okay with you?" he asked.

Melody made an agreeable sort of sound just as Vince Gill started singing a love ballad over the radio. The air in the truck was heavy, probably due to the clouds churning overhead. "Mmm," she whispered, closing her eyes. "It almost smells like carnations in here."

"Flowers," he said quietly. "Everything happened so fast I completely forgot about flowers."

"That's all right. I understand."

"You really are being great about this," he answered, visibly relaxing.

"What's the matter? Aren't wives usually this understanding?"

While Vince Gill hit a high note on the radio, Clayt's voice rang out deep and clear. "I've only had one other wife, and no one ever accused Victoria of being understanding."

Melody listened very hard for any hint of leftover feelings Clayt might have for his former wife. Hearing none, she said, "What ever happened between you and Victoria? I mean, one minute you seemed madly in love with her, and the next you were getting a divorce."

Clayt slowed down as he came to the outskirts of Jasper Gulch. Cletus McCully would be sitting on his usual bench in front of the post office this time of the day, and at least a handful of other locals would be shooting the breeze in front of the barbershop. Since nobody else knew that he and Mel had eloped, he turned a corner and made his way to the alley behind the diner by way of another street.

"Clayt?"

There went that butterfly touch of her hand again. And there went that zing all the way through him. "You don't really want to talk about Victoria, do you?" he asked, covering her hand with his own.

Melody's breath caught in her throat at the huskiness in Clayt's voice. He pulled to a stop in the alley and threw the gearshift into Neutral.

"As long as you aren't thinking of confessing that you're still in love with her, I guess I don't need to hear about her," she said dreamily.

His gaze roamed her face, homing in on her mouth. Melody's insides were turning to liquid, her vision blurring as he slowly brought his face closer. In a voice barely more than a whisper, he said, "Good, because aside from the fact that she's Haley's mother, I can't think of much good to say about her. I got over her a long time ago. I suppose I thought I was in love with her once, but now I know it was only desire. And speaking of desire..."

Before she could make sense of the warning bells going off inside her head, he covered her lips with his. The next thing she knew he was gathering her in his arms, his hands gliding down her back, fitting her tight to his body. She moaned his name on a deep sigh. When his hand inched between their bodies and covered her breast, she stopped breathing altogether.

His hand kneaded and caressed. Of its own volition, her back arched into his touch. He dragged his mouth away from hers and sucked in a ragged breath. Her head tipped back, her eyes drifting open.

"I know," he said, as if reading the surprise in her expression. "This is as big a shock to me as it is to you."

He kissed her again. The next thing she knew, she was

standing in the alley, watching him drive away. He lowered his window at the last second, the look he gave her nearly buckling her knees all over again.

"You're coming to the ranch tonight, right?"

"Just like we planned," she said.

A muscle worked in his jaw again, but he smiled, and in a voice deep and laden with desire, he said, "I'll see you then."

Melody watched him drive away. Something bothered the back of her mind, but with her head still spinning, she couldn't put her finger on what it was. Blaming her misgivings on nerves and excitement, she hurried into the diner where the supper crowd would be gathering soon.

It was almost dark by the time she pointed her car down the road that led to the Carson place two miles west of town. It had taken her twice as long to clean up the kitchen and put up the chairs and sweep the floor. Maybe if she'd been more experienced it would be different. Surely all women were nervous when they were about to lose their virginity.

She slammed on the brakes so hard her tires slid over the loose gravel. She had to calm down. She'd nearly burned the meat loaf, and when Boomer Brown had asked for a refill, she'd filled his saucer along with his coffee cup. More than one customer had asked her if anything was wrong. Feeling the simple gold ring in her pocket, she'd pasted on a smile and had shaken her head.

That very afternoon she'd married the man she'd been in love with most of her life. What could possibly be wrong?

Clayt and Haley both looked up from the corral when she pulled into the driveway. Even General Custer, Clayt's cattle dog, was standing by the edge of the corral looking decidedly ill at ease.

Oh-oh. Maybe something had gone wrong after all.

* * *

"You what?" Haley sputtered.

Clayt fought the urge to swipe his hat off his head and run his fingers through his hair. Since he didn't want Haley to pick up on any uncertainties he was feeling, he held the filly's reins and brought her horse to a stop. Glancing up at Haley, he said, "You heard me. Mel and I got married this afternoon."

They both turned at the sound of a car pulling to a stop in the middle of the driveway. Clayt felt a grin slide across his face as Mel climbed out of her car and closed the door. If Haley hadn't been sitting in the saddle on a horse that was decidedly jumpy, he would have swiped his hat off his head and tossed it straight into the air.

Mel McCully—make that Mel Carson—was his bride. His wife.

The knowledge worked over him on a wave of need. The hot jolt of desire had come as quite a shock the first time he'd experienced it. It had happened so often these past few weeks he was coming to expect it. And honestly, he would have to be crazy to mind the sensation.

Haley dismounted the way he'd taught her. Eyes narrowed, lips pursed, she strode to the fence.

He'd been looking for a good mother figure for Haley. As far as he was concerned, a healthy sex life was going to be an added bonus. Ooo-eee, he thought as the same wind that plastered his shirt to his back ruffled Mel's shirt against her breasts. A healthy sex life would be an added bonus indeed.

Melody glanced at Clayt as she neared. His jeans were faded, his belt worn, his boots scuffed. His stance was one of a true cowboy, hands on hips, feet spread a comfortable distance apart, chin raised at a lofty angle. His brown hat shaded his eyes, making them appear dark, dark gray beneath the glow of the mercury light high on the barn. Clayt Carson had never been prone to smiles, but the way his lips lifted in the corners made her pretty sure he was glad to see her. His daughter was another story.

"Hi, Haley."

Silence.

"Have you named your horse yet?"

The girl's answer was reluctant at best. "I named her Snooks. It's what Mama used to call me when I was small."

Holding Haley's gaze, Melody nodded and strolled to the fence where she hiked one boot onto a low board. "That's a good name. I once had a horse named Toots. You know, like foots only with a *T*. He was the biggest flirt on the planet."

The little girl made no comment. She might have had her mother's eye color and pert nose, but in that instant she reminded Melody more of Clayt. Maybe it was the set of her chin or the squint of her eyes or the way she held her shoulders as if she'd gladly take on the world.

"You're dying to ask, Haley. You might as well go ahead."

The child's eyes opened wide for a moment. By the time she cast her father a long glance and met Melody's eyes again, she'd recovered. "Clayton says you two got married today. I don't believe him."

It was Melody's turn to glance at Clayt. He shrugged before striding the remaining few steps to the fence.

"Has your father ever lied to you before?" Melody asked.

Haley shook her head slowly in the gathering darkness.

"Then why don't you believe him?"

"Because," she said, raising her little chin haughtily, "when people get married all they do is kiss. Look at Uncle Luke and Aunt Jillian. Wyatt and Lisa kiss all the time, too. And just yesterday Jeremy Everts and I saw Boomer and DoraLee in a liplock in front of the Crazy Horse. How can you be married when you don't even kiss?''

Melody and Clayt shared a meaningful look, but Clayt was the only one who moved. His boots creaked and his shirt rustled, his eyes delving into hers as he rested his big hand on her arm. As if by unspoken agreement, he lowered his face as she raised hers. The meeting of their lips couldn't have been more perfectly choreographed or more perfectly timed.

Melody tried to remind herself the kiss was just for show. Surely they'd both intended it to be an act, but the instant her lips opened beneath his, everything changed. He smelled of man and wind and wide open spaces, his lips firm and masculine and amazingly primal. The hand on her arm tightened; the fingers of his other hand slid into her hair. Her body warmed and her senses spun, making her thankful for the hold she had on the wooden fence.

General Custer, Clayt's faithful old dog, howled. Sounding thoroughly disgusted, Haley said, ''Come on, General, let's go in the house.''

''Haley,'' Clayt said, turning to look at his daughter, ''General Custer isn't allowed inside.''

''I know, I know.''

Watching Haley lope toward the house, the black-and-white dog at her side, Melody said, ''I think it's safe to say she believes us.''

Clayt's silence drew Melody's face around. He was looking at her mouth, and he wasn't even trying to disguise his need or his intentions. Suddenly Melody felt as if she were in over her head.

She glanced at the old white house, and then at her car. Ducking her head, her brief flirtation with shyness, she said, ''I guess I'll get my bag.''

"If you wait a few minutes for me to get Snooks tucked in for the night, I'll go with you."

"That's okay," she said, spinning around. "I think I'll go in and check on Haley."

She reached her car in record time. Suitcase in hand, she hurried toward the house, patting General Custer's head on her way by. Once inside, she leaned against the door and took a deep breath.

Haley must have turned on the lights on her way through, but she was nowhere in sight. Nerves churned in Melody's stomach and danced up and down her spine. She walked through the kitchen and into the living room where an old sofa and an easy chair faced a television. There was an open staircase on the far wall. Beyond that was the doorway that led to Clayt's bedroom.

Swallowing, she clutched the handle of her suitcase and inched her way into the room. One of Clayt's shirts hung over a chair, two pairs of his boots were lined up against the wall nearby. The furniture had probably been in this room for generations, but the mattress looked thick and new. Melody sank to the edge of the bed. Feeling her cheeks color, she covered them with her hands and glanced at her reflection in the mirror across the room. Her hands fell away from her face. Alone, she could let her guard down, her shoulders droop. She was a married woman. What in God's name was she supposed to do next?

She was on her feet, across the room, and out the door before she could blink. She didn't stop until she found Haley's room upstairs.

The girl was sitting on the floor, toying with the fringe on a pair of chaps. Without looking up, she said, "Why did you have to go and marry Clayton?"

Melody chose her words carefully. "You asked me to help you. Would you have been happier if he'd have married Pamela Sue?"

The child crossed her eyes and stuck out her tongue. "It doesn't matter." Which, of course, meant that it did. Rubbing at a scuff mark on her boot, she said, "What am I supposed to call you now?"

"Melody would be nice."

Haley shrugged as if it was all the same to her. In a voice that had gone softer, she said, "He used to kiss Mama like that, you know."

Melody didn't know why that bothered her, but it did. Sitting on the edge of Haley's twin bed, she said, "Were you hoping your mother and father would get back together some day?"

Haley shook her head. "Mama says he's uncouth."

If Melody hadn't been an adult, she would have crossed her eyes and stuck out her tongue, too.

"Why'd you really marry him?"

Melody didn't know what to say or how much to tell Haley, so she simply lowered her voice and told her the truth. "I love him, Haley."

The girl's eyes raised to hers and seemed to say, "Yeah? And who loves me?"

Before Melody could think of any way to put the girl's fears to rest, Haley said, "I think I'll go to bed now."

"All right. I'll see you in the morning."

She couldn't quite make out Haley's reply.

Clayt was hanging his hat by the back door when Melody descended the last step. He looked at her across the span of two rooms, his eyes taking on that sleepy glint that didn't necessarily mean he was sleepy. He strolled closer, all cowboy swagger and pure masculine brawn.

"Is Haley taking it okay?" he asked.

Shrugging, Melody said, "For now. But I doubt we've heard the last of it."

He took another step toward her and raised his right hand. Doing a quick sidestep, she skirted the sofa and eluded his advance. "Clayt," she said, twisting the afghan on the back of the sofa.

"Hmm?"

Something was bothering her, and she swore it was more than just nerves. Unfortunately she wasn't going to figure it out as long as Clayt was looking at her like that. Clasping her hands together to still a nervous flutter, she said, "Why don't you go up and say good-night to Haley. I think I'm going to take a long, hot bath."

"All right," he said, smiling slowly. "Take all the time you need. I'll be right here when you're ready."

Gulp.

If he was trying to put her at ease, it wasn't working.

She ducked into the bedroom for her nightgown then made a beeline for the bathroom. Turning the old-fashioned lock on the door, she sank to the edge of the claw-footed bathtub and started the water. By the time she turned the faucets off and sank into the blessedly hot water, she could hear Clayt's voice on the other side of the painted wooden door. It sounded as if he was talking on the phone.

"Yeah, little Mel McCully...I know...I know Victoria and I married on the spur of the moment, too. Believe me, Dad, this is completely different."

So. He was talking to his parents. There was no reason for that to bother her. Yet something was making the niggling doubt in the back of her mind grow bigger. And it had something to do with Victoria.

"Yeah, she's great with Haley. I know. I remember. Sure, Dad, put Mom on."

When the bathwater turned lukewarm, Melody pulled the plug, dried herself off and donned her knee-skimming white nightgown and her long terry robe. The television was on when she opened the bathroom door, but most of the lights throughout the house were dim. Finding the coast clear, she slipped out of the bathroom. She was halfway through the living room when Clayt's voice sounded behind her.

"My parents send their love and best wishes."

She spun around, her robe swishing around her ankles. Clayt had removed his shirt and boots. Bare, his shoulders looked broad, his chest well-defined, the muscles down his stomach as rippled as a washboard.

Melody felt herself going warm inside, her bones turning to liquid, her thoughts slowing. "Then your parents weren't upset?"

He walked closer, shaking his head. "My mother said I should have married you ten years ago."

She'd had no idea she was walking backward until she felt the mattress on the backs of her legs. Clayt had followed her, his eyes never leaving her face. "Maybe she's right," he said quietly.

Ten years ago he'd married Victoria. Melody would never forget that day, because that was the day she'd almost left Jasper Gulch. She remembered standing at one end of Main Street, staring at the dusty street, the faded awnings and painted storefronts, thinking about her future. Her grandfather was getting on in years, her parents had been gone for a long time, and the man she loved had married somebody else. Her best friend was moving to Aberdeen. Mel had considered going along. For some reason her gaze had trailed to the diner that had been closed for almost a year. The McCully pluck had returned in full force, and she'd known what she wanted to do. She only wished her instincts would tell her what to do now.

"Clayt, we have to talk."

He took another step. "I know. There are a lot of things we haven't discussed. I know running the diner takes a lot of your time. Don't worry, I don't expect you to do everything around here. We'll both have some adjustments to make, but I'll do my level best to make things as easy for you as possible.'' His gaze dropped from her eyes, to her mouth, to her breasts. ''By the way, what side of the bed do you like to sleep on?''

''Clayt,'' she said again.

''What's the matter? Are you the type who takes her half out of the middle?''

''No. Umm…that is.''

''Mel, you don't have to be nervous. I know it's your first time.''

She didn't have the presence of mind to be offended. He was strolling toward her, taking one giant step for every small backward step of hers. ''If it's any consolation,'' he said, his voice so low she swore she could feel its vibration on the tops of her bare feet, ''it's been a long time for me, too. There's been a noted lack of women in these parts, you know.''

''Yes.'' She wet her lips. ''I know.''

His slow, smooth grin nearly buckled her knees. Before he could take another step, the niggling doubt in the back of her mind moved front and center. An instant later it dawned on her what was wrong. Clayt had told her that desire was the only thing that had been between him and Victoria. As far as he was concerned, desire was the only thing between Clayt and *her.*

If desire hadn't turned into love with Victoria, what made her think it would be any different with *her?* She'd saved her virginity for almost thirty years. Was she really ready to lose it to a man who wanted her but didn't love her? Earlier, when Clayt had kissed her, she'd thought going to bed with her husband was the next logical thing to do. Everything had happened so fast. She hadn't had time to think things through. She wanted Clayt's desire, but she wanted his love, too. And she didn't think she could settle for one without the other. She was afraid that going to bed with him too soon would allow Clayt to believe what was between them was simple. She wanted love between them. And it seemed that love was rarely simple.

"Clayt," she said, determination inching its way back into her voice.

His hair was a dark, dark brown, his eyes deep and sensual and all male. "Do you have any idea what my name looks like uttered on your lips?"

She sucked in a shallow breath. "I think you've gotten the wrong idea about tonight."

"Honey, I only have one idea for tonight, and I don't see how it could be wrong."

If she didn't put an end to this in the next second, she never would. Forcing her confused emotions in order, she said, "Stop right there."

Clayt's heart was chugging like a freight train, but the sound inside his head was more like the bong of a Chinese gong. Mel had stopped backing up and was no longer clutching her collar to her throat like a virgin of old. Her eyes were flashing, and her hand was held up in a halting motion.

"I agreed to marry you because of Haley," she said. "I never said I'd sleep with you."

Bong. Bong. Bong.

"What are you trying to say?" he asked through the roaring din in his ears.

Her eyes darted away shyly, only to light on his once again. "Everything has happened so fast we haven't had time to discuss the details of our marriage."

"The details." He knew his voice had hardened, but he couldn't help it. He hadn't been this worked up in a long time and, dammit, he was in no mood to talk.

"Yes, the details," she said, gesturing toward the doorway. "This old house has more bedrooms. I think it would be better if I slept in one of them."

His eyes pinned her to the spot. "We're married. And married people sleep in the same room, in the same bed."

"We got married because Haley needs a mother."

"What about that kiss out by the corral?"

She raised her chin a notch. "Wasn't that for Haley's sake, too?"

Now that he'd gotten his breathing under control, he gathered his wits about him enough to take a long, hard look at Mel. It was true that they hadn't discussed this.

He'd just assumed...

He'd thought...

Aw, hell.

Mel was looking at him much the way she'd looked at him that day all those years ago when she'd kicked him in the shin. Her blue eyes flashed, her chin was raised haughtily, and her nostrils flared. She might call herself Melody. And her last name was now Carson. But she was still the same ornery, cantankerous female she'd always been.

Cursing under his breath, he reached for his boots with one hand and his shirt with the other.

"Clayt, where are you going?"

He took a moment to pull on his boots and shrug into his shirt, but he didn't look at her when he said, "I need some air."

His long strides practically burned up the worn carpet and old vinyl kitchen floor. If it hadn't rained last month, he would have started a grass fire in his own side yard. He breathed in the cool, damp night air and heaved a saddle onto his favorite horse. Glancing over his shoulder at the light in his own bedroom window, he swore all over again.

He hoisted one boot into the stirrup and scowled at the pull of his jeans. Cramming his hat on his head, he swung onto Rambler's back. The horse reared up, then took off down the lane at a gallop.

The cold wind stung Clayt's face, but it was a long time

before his mind was clear enough to permit rational thinking. Keeping his jaw clenched and his hold on the reins tight, he supposed he shouldn't have been surprised that Mel wasn't going to make things easy. She'd been a royal pain since she'd kicked him all those years ago. Although the pain he was feeling now was slightly higher, it was no less intense.

Clenching his teeth until his jaw ached, he pressed Rambler to go faster. It seemed that neither his anger nor the sting of the cool autumn air had the effect on his body he'd hoped for. There was only one thing that would relieve so much need. And Mel had decided to sleep in the spare room.

Confounded, ill-tempered, cantankerous woman.

"Good morning, Haley," Melody said, pouring herself a cup of coffee.

The child mumbled something under her breath and reached for a box of cold cereal.

"I have time to fix you a bowl of oatmeal before I leave for the diner."

"Don't want any."

Leaning against the counter, Melody eyed the girl over the top of her coffee cup. Haley was wearing purple jeans, a plain white T-shirt and tennis shoes with orange laces. Her hair appeared to have been freshly combed, and her face had probably been washed. It was hard to tell with her chin tucked so close to her chest. Haley Carson was sulking. When the door opened and Clayt stomped into the kitchen, it became apparent that she wasn't the only one.

"Coffee's hot," she said, holding up her own mug.

A muscle worked in Clayt's jaw when he met her look. For a moment Melody thought he might give in and smile, but he jerked his eyes away and reached for a cup, and the moment passed. He strode to the refrigerator and retrieved a slice of bologna from its package then proceeded to slap it between two slices of bread and stuff the whole thing into a plastic bag for Haley's lunch. Adding a few store-bought cookies, he glanced at the clock on the stove and said, "The bus will be here any minute, Haley."

"I can take you to school," Melody said to Haley. "It's right on my way."

The girl was shaking her head before Melody had finished speaking. With a slurp of milk and the clatter of her spoon, Haley said, "Jeremy Everts is bringing a frog to school today. We hafta make plans."

Haley clamped her mouth shut, her eyes growing huge as her father took an ominous step closer. Holding out her lunch, he said, "I don't want you getting into any trouble at school today. Understand?"

She nodded slowly, but when she reached for her lunch with one hand and her backpack with the other, it was obvious that she thought her whole day was shot. Shoulders slumped and chin down, she headed for the back door. Clayt and Melody both called goodbye, and then they were alone.

They looked at each other, but neither of them seemed to know what to say. He looked tired this morning, and even more sullen than usual. She'd been awake when he'd come in shortly after midnight. The house was sturdy, but it was old...the floors creaking beneath every step he took. She'd held her breath at the sound of his boots on the stairs and had almost cried out when her door had creaked open. She didn't know how long he stood there, and she didn't know why. She only knew that she wasn't sure she could have said no to him a second time. When he'd turned and made his way back downstairs, her heart had swelled with feeling. Clayt Carson could act like an ornery rogue, but underneath he was a very honorable man.

She'd lain awake for a long time after that, thinking.

Clayt had married her. And it was up to her to see to it that he wasn't sorry. In order to do that, she was going to have to find a way to make him love her. One of her grandfather's favorite sayings about stubbornness had filtered through her mind. *You can lead a horse to water, but you can't make it drink.*

Clayt Carson was as stubborn as they came.

Searching for some way to break the ice this morning, Melody asked, "What are you planning to do today?"

He leaned against the counter and crossed his ankles, but he spoke without meeting her eyes. "The drought had its way with the hay crop." He swallowed, grimacing at his choice of words. After clearing his throat, he said, "Anyway, this morning somebody's supposed to deliver two semi loads of hay I ordered. Jason Tucker and I are going to unload it and stack it in the barn for winter."

"It sounds like hard work."

He turned his head as she turned hers. "I don't mind hard work, Mel, and although we didn't get off to a real good start last night, I intend to be a good husband. I'll work hard and be the best provider I can be. I guess what I'm trying to say is this. If you tell me what you want, I'll try to get it for you."

Melody gave him a soft smile and swallowed the lump in her throat. There was only one thing she wanted. So far, he'd failed to offer her that.

"Well," she said when the silence had stretched about as far as it could between them. "I guess I'd better get to work."

He didn't kiss her goodbye. He didn't even smile. Five hours later Melody was still telling herself she wasn't disappointed.

She shouldn't have had time to be disappointed, as busy as she'd been all morning. The lunch crowd was extra boisterous and hungry. It was all she and Louetta could do to keep up with them.

"Whew," Louetta declared, setting her tray on the counter in the diner's old kitchen. "Just when I think things are slowing down a new batch of people comes in. Forrest Wilkie wants a hot chicken sandwich, an order of coleslaw and a slice of cherry pie. I still need two orders of fries and two burgers for Lisa and Wyatt, and three potpies for the Anderson brothers. Karl Hanson wants more coffee. Oh, and DoraLee wants to know if you're okay."

Melody turned around in time to see Louetta untie her apron and hang it over a towel bar near the sink. The other woman's cheeks were rosy; tendrils of hair that had escaped the knot at her nape waving around her face. "Louetta, where are you going?"

"Mother and Isabell came face-to-face only moments ago. Isabell glared, and mother left in tears. I hate to do this to you, Melody, but I really have to leave for a few minutes. I'll be back as soon as I calm Mother down."

Melody perked up despite her fatigue and her worries. Until a month ago, Isabell Pruitt and Opal Graham had been best friends all their lives. Although folks had been dying to know what had caused the rift, nobody really had a clue. After all, Isabell and Opal were the two biggest gossips in Jasper Gulch. And their lips were sealed.

"Isabell's still here?" Melody asked.

Louetta nodded. "She's sitting at her usual table. Don't forget Forrest's pie and Karl Hanson's coffee."

"I won't. Give your mother my best, and hurry back." She turned, only to discover that she was talking to herself. Louetta had already gone.

Tucking her hair into the big barrette she now wore instead of her long braid, Melody went to work filling the orders Louetta had taken. She balanced the heavy tray on one hand and one shoulder and pushed through the swinging door. The place was full. Even the booths were occupied today, which was unusual, since folks didn't come to the diner for privacy.

She served all the lunches, then walked around with a steaming carafe of coffee. She was halfway around the room when Roy Everts mentioned that his grandson Jeremy had gotten sent home from school for putting a frog in Amy Wilkie's desk. "His mama's fit to be tied. Last month he went skinny-dippin' with Haley Carson. And now this. I don't know what's come over that boy."

Isabell raised what little chin she had and self-righteously said, "Haley Carson's what's come over him, that's what."

Melody filled Boomer Brown's cup, hoping the topic would turn to something else. She wasn't that lucky. Edith Ferguson was nodding the way she always did when she was preparing to speak her mind. "That's right. Jenny Jacobs told me that Mertyl Gentry said that Phyllis O'Grady, who lives next door to Jeremy, told her that Haley Carson not only went skinny-dipping with Jeremy. She stole his clothes, too. The poor child had to hide in a briar patch until Wyatt McCully brought him his clothes. Why, that girl's a heathen."

"She's been through a lot," someone else said.

"Children have been known to go through worse things."

"That's right. She needs a spanking, that's what she needs."

"I heard that Clayton is looking to find a new mother for Haley," Phyllis said in a whisper that could have penetrated steel.

Isabell pounded her bony fist on the table. "Who on God's green earth would be foolish enough to take on that job?"

"For your information," Mel declared, "somebody already has."

Chapter Seven

Melody stopped short.

What had she said? What had she done?

She and Clayt hadn't even told their families that they were married, and here she'd practically blurted it to some of the biggest gossips in Jasper Gulch. If her hands hadn't been full she would have covered her mouth. Feeling like a deer trapped in the glare of headlights, her eyes darted over people she'd known all her life. Part of her wished the floor would swallow her whole, while another part of her wanted to empty her coffee carafe in Isabell's soup.

A movement near the kitchen drew her gaze. She stared wordlessly as Clayt came toward her. A buzz started in one end of the diner. Melody barely heard. All her attention was trained on the expression deep in Clayt's eyes.

"What's going on?" somebody asked.

"Why, I believe our Mel is implying that somebody has agreed to become Haley Carson's stepmother."

"Who?"

"The Southern belle with the big—ow!" one of the men

said, rubbing his arm where it had been duly jabbed by his wife's sharp elbow.

"Folks," Clayt said, keeping his eyes on Mel. "We have an announcement to make."

"What does he mean *we*?"

"If you'd shut up for half a minute we all might find out."

"Who are you telling to shut up?"

"Shh. I can't hear."

The murmur chasing through the room turned into a hushed stillness when Clayt stopped a few feet from Mel. She was watching him, blank, shaken and obviously tongue-tied, but her blue eyes also glowed with intelligence and an inner fire he was only now coming to recognize. Removing his hat with his thumb and forefinger, he said, "Honey, do you want to tell 'em, or should I?"

Melody looked up at him and smiled. "I guess it's a little late to make Granddad the next person to know, but it seems fitting somehow that we tell my patrons first. Go ahead, Clayt. I'd like you to do the honors."

He'd known this woman all his life, but he swore he'd never heard her voice so soft and sultry and so laden with desire. He paused, realization dawning. That's what her voice had been. Laden with desire. For him.

"Sugar," DoraLee said from a table on the other side of the room, "if one of you doesn't say something pretty soon, we're all just gonna die from curiosity."

Clayt felt his loftiness return in one rousing swoop. He didn't know what last night had been about, but whether Mel admitted it or not, she wanted him. He aimed to give her what she wanted. But first he had a little announcement to make.

"Folks," he said, reaching for Mel's hand. "Mel and I paid a little visit to the justice of the peace in Murdo."

"You eloped?"

"You mean you and Mel got married?"

"Without telling anybody?"

"Well I'll be gol-darned."

Melody and Clayt looked at each other while voices they both recognized swirled all around them. DoraLee was suddenly in front of them, hugging them both at the same time, Boomer right behind her.

"How long you two been hitched?" Boomer asked.

"Since yesterday," Mel answered.

"No wonder you look tired today," DoraLee said with a wink and a smile.

Isabell made a pained sound, and Melody shot a glance at Clayt. He didn't dispute DoraLee's assumption. Instead, he looked at her, his eyes full of sexual intent and male appreciation and maybe even a little admiration.

"Shoot," one of the Anderson brothers declared. "That means Mel-o-dy's off the market."

"Yeah," one of his brothers agreed. "But if Clayt's a married man, somebody's gonna have to console Pamela Sue, and I aim to be that somebody."

"Get in line."

"Right after me."

It looked as if poor Pamela Sue wasn't going to be lonely for long.

Melody smiled up at Clayt. "I didn't know you were coming into town today."

He seemed to have a difficult time pulling his eyes away from her mouth. When he finally succeeded, his voice was deeper, and that lofty glint was back in his eyes. "I'm mighty glad I stopped by."

"Why did you stop by, Clayt?"

He motioned toward the kitchen where they could talk in private. When they'd reached the other side of the swinging door, he said, "It occurred to me that I might have been a tad on the ornery side this morning."

Melody knew better than to touch that line. Clayt Carson was a *tad* ornery like he was a *tad* rugged or a *tad* tall. Folding her arms, she looked up at him and waited for him to continue.

"I'm driving out to check on the herd west of Stoney Creek this afternoon. I want to look things over so I can decide how many calves to keep and how many feeders I'm going to ship next month. I've hired a sitter to stay with Haley when she gets out of school. I should be back before dark, and I was just thinking that that's about the time you'll probably be getting home."

Was it her imagination or had he moved closer?

"Home?" she asked.

His face blurred before her eyes. The next thing she knew, he was kissing her. His reaction was swift and violent while hers was slower, but no less intense. Her pulse beat at the base of her throat, and her heart felt too large for her chest. And lower, she felt a tingling sensation, and a slow, swaying pull she'd never felt before.

He lifted his face from hers, and darned if he didn't grin. "I'd say it's going to be a long afternoon, wouldn't you?"

He put his hat on his head, granted her another of his rare smiles, and sauntered out the back door. Mel was left standing there, the ruckus in the next room barely discernible over the erratic thud of her heart.

Clayt had gone along with the sleeping arrangements last night. Something told her that tonight things were going to be a lot different.

Clayt swiped his hat from his head and wiped his brow with the back of his hand. He was standing in the back of his pickup truck, his eyes squinting as they swept the horizon where a herd of brown and white cattle were foraging for grass. It was almost October, and the days were getting shorter, the skies churning up gray clouds that would soon be spitting snow. The rain last month had saved the grass on the plains from burning up completely, but it had come too late to do much good for this year. The oat and hay crops in the area hadn't fared much better, which meant that more hay and feed was going to have to be trucked in, and more calves were going to have to be shipped to feeders out East. Winters were harsh out here and seemed to come earlier every year. This one was going to be leaner than most.

His stomach rumbled with hunger, but it wasn't much competition for the other hunger deep inside him. A need had been building in him for weeks. The knowledge that Mel felt a similar need only made it stronger.

Placing one hand on the side of the truck, he vaulted to the ground. Hoisting a salt lick in each hand, he dropped them in strategic places near the watering holes. He'd nearly finished what he'd gone out there to do when an old pickup truck chugged toward him down the lane.

"Boy," Cletus McCully said, stepping stiffly down from the cab of his truck.

Clayt rubbed the day's dirt from his hands before placing them on his hips. The old man hiked his pants higher on his waist and ambled closer on legs bowed from all the years he'd spent in a saddle.

"I just heard you eloped with my granddaughter."

"That's right."

"Noticed ya didn't bother to ask me for Mel's hand."

Cletus McCully never had been one to beat around the bush. Nodding, Clayt said, "You know Mel, Cletus. She knows her own mind as well as you know yours."

Cletus harrumphed and snapped one suspender beneath the open lapels of his coat. Peering up at Clayt through craggy white brows, the old man said, "If you're tellin' me Mel's stubborn, don't waste your breath. She comes by it naturally. But she's been my little girl since the day we buried her mama and daddy. You're a good cattle man, Clayton. You know horses, too. It just so happens that I think a lot of you. Always have. That don't mean there won't be hell to pay if you hurt her.''

Clayt nodded. Having said what he'd come to say, Cletus crammed his shabby old hat on his head and headed back toward his truck. Cows lowed, and more than one calf bawled as the old man drove away. Clayt stayed where he was until Cletus's truck had disappeared over the rolling hills in the distance.

Heading for the cab of his own truck, Clayt thought about Mel's grandfather. Cletus's voice might have held an ominous ring, but he'd be back to his old self by morning, swapping stories with his cronies in front of the post office, complaining about taxes and the weather, not necessarily in that order. Yes, by morning, Cletus would be back to his old self. By morning, Clayt was going to be a married man in every sense of the word.

He didn't know what last night had been about. Maybe it was like Cletus had said and Mel was just stubborn, or maybe she'd been nervous. But he'd felt her desire unfold like petals on a flower that very afternoon. Nervous or not, there wasn't anything that was going to keep her out of his bed tonight.

In deference to Cletus and to Mel herself, he vowed to do his level best to love her slow and easy the first time. He wasn't guaranteeing anything after that.

The lights were on in his house when he rounded the last curve in the lane. It was after eight, and Mel's car was sitting in the driveway. He'd forgotten how inviting lighted windows could be. He'd forgotten how it felt to know a woman was waiting for him, too. He planned to take a quick hot shower, grab a bite to eat and spend a little time with Haley. And then, after his daughter was asleep, the night would be his and Mel's.

"I'm home," he called.

The kitchen was empty, and so was the living room. "Mel? Haley?"

He'd already started to take the stairs two at a time when Mel's voice halted him where he stood. "Before you talk to Haley, I have to tell you something."

He turned around. His eyes took their time meeting hers, traveling over her faded jeans and long-sleeved shirt, settling momentarily on her parted lips, letting her know he was thinking about kissing her, among other things.

"Clayt," she said, wetting her lips in a way that only increased his need.

He ambled a little closer and slanted her his best killer smile. "Uh, Mel? You might be getting cold feet again, but I can make you warm and pliant if you'll just give me the chance."

Her cheeks colored and her throat constricted, but she sucked in a quick breath, her eyes going all soft and dewy and deep. Retracing his steps to the middle of the room where Mel was standing, he said, "I've been thinking about taking a quick shower and grabbing a bite to eat. If Haley isn't awake, I'd just as soon skip supper. How about you?"

Melody breathed deeply, inhaling the scent of hay and wind and clothes left outside to dry. Her gaze did a slow climb up Clayt's chest, past the tanned column of his neck. He had a square jaw and a mouth that was made for rakish grins. His bottom lip was slightly thicker than the top, the corners meeting the shallow creases in his lean cheeks.

Her heart was beating an erratic rhythm, and she knew there was something she was supposed to tell him. Vaguely she even remembered that she wasn't supposed to allow herself to settle for desire and nothing more. But the way Clayt was looking at her brought out a yearning so incredible she thought she might go up in smoke if he didn't kiss her soon.

"Melody, did ya tell him yet?" Haley's voice drifted down the stairs, stopping the downward motion of Clayt's head and the upward tilt of hers.

"Clayt," Melody said again, "there's something I have to tell you."

Looking slightly dazed, he said, "You aren't going to tell me that you haven't moved your things downstairs, are you?"

She shook her head. She'd brought another load of her things with her tonight and she'd put them in his room.

"Good." The word came out as slow and deep as a midnight sigh. "Because, Mel?" he whispered in case Haley was listening, "I've been waiting to get you alone behind a closed door all day."

Grimacing slightly, she said, "I'm afraid we aren't exactly going to be alone."

Something moved at the very edge of Clayt's peripheral vision. General Custer, the best cow dog Clayt had ever had, whined from the bedroom doorway.

Clayt turned his head, his mouth dropping open at the sight awaiting him. "What happened to the General? Where's his fur?"

"That's what I've been trying to tell you. Haley sheared him."

"You mean like a sheep?"

Melody ducked her head. "More like a billiard ball."

Clayt was in his bedroom in three strides. General Custer had always behaved with a kind of dignity that was almost human. Right now he was looking up at Clayt out of the tops of his eyes as if he'd been caught naked in a crowded room.

Clayt went down on his haunches and ran a hand over

what was left of a thick black-and-white coat. "Aw, General."

"It'll grow back," Mel said behind him.

"Haley did this?" He glanced up at Mel. Suddenly feeling inept at raising his own child, he asked, "Why?"

"We both knew we hadn't heard the last from her concerning our marriage," Melody said quietly. "She's too young to go on strike or burn her bra or sit us down and tell us how she feels about our marriage."

"You mean she was making a statement?"

Mel nodded. "She was letting us know where she stands."

Clayt ran a hand through his hair. "Why couldn't she just throw a temper tantrum like other kids?"

"That's not her way."

"But I love that dog."

"Haley loves him, too," Mel said. "I think she's trying to determine how much you love *her*."

Suddenly Clayt felt the way he had the night Wyatt brought Haley home after catching her in the act of stealing brownies off Lisa's front porch. In the old days a father would have handled the situation by taking a little trip out behind the woodshed with the naughty child. A lot of professionals had come up with new theories on discipline since then. Clayt could have used an expert's opinion right now. "What do you think we should do?"

Mel was looking at him as if she fully understood his feelings of inadequacy where Haley was concerned. Shrugging, she said, "Although she won't admit it, I think she feels Victoria's abandonment all the way to her soul."

"Then spanking's out, huh?"

Mel nodded. "We have to let her know that there's nothing she can do to lose our love."

General Custer shivered beneath Clayt's hand. "What about the General?"

"He can sleep in here until his fur grows back."

"He's not sleeping in here, Mel."

She raised her eyebrows but kept her voice quiet. "He seems to have chosen this room. Do you want to be the one to tell him different?"

General Custer looked up at Clayt with eyes older than time. Remembering all the stray cattle the dog had rounded up and all the long days he'd worked for nothing more than a meal and a few kind words, Clayt couldn't quite bring himself to order the faithful dog to leave. He supposed he didn't have a problem with the General sleeping in his room, as long as Mel slept there, too.

"Clayton?" Haley called from the next room.

"You might as well come in," he said.

The girl inched her way as far as the doorway. She stood with one foot tucked under her flannel nightgown, looking lost and forlorn and so darn sorry it made his heart swell. "Do you think General Custer hates me?"

Clayt had a feeling she was really asking him if he did. "I think he's disappointed and embarrassed and maybe a little sad, but if you explain things to him and are extra nice, he'll forgive you."

She heaved a sigh too large for a girl her age. "I think he'd like it if I slept in here with him so he won't be scared."

Clayt glanced at Mel, who was sitting on the edge of the bed. His bed.

Those Chinese gongs were going off inside his skull again. He glanced back at Haley, who was looking at him with big brown eyes that were full of entreaty and trust and hope. General Custer looked up at him as if he fully expected Clayt to do the right thing.

Aw, hell.

Heaving a sigh that was even bigger than Haley's had been, he nodded. Mel smiled at him from her perch on the bed, a pulse beating at the base of her neck. He shook his head slowly. He finally had her in his bed, and it didn't look as if there was going to be room for him.

"All right, Haley," he said, opening his arms to his little girl. "You can sleep in here with the General, but only for tonight."

"Only for tonight," she said, snuggling into his arms. "I promise."

Five days later Clayt was fit to be tied. Haley had been behaving marvelously. Even her teacher had called to inform him of his daughter's apparent change in attitude. She was getting along better with the other children, and she seemed to be adjusting to the third grade. "Whatever you're doing," Mrs. Moore had said, "don't change it."

Every night the whole family assembled in the bedroom downstairs. To Clayt it felt ridiculously like being in a Norman Rockwell painting: Mel's hair spread over the pillow in the moonlight, Haley curled into a ball at their feet, the General snoring peacefully on the rug on the floor. Night after night Clayt stared at the ceiling, willing his body to relax. Night after night his body had other ideas. When he couldn't stand another minute of *not* sleeping, and *not* doing anything else, he crept upstairs where he crawled into a spare bed. By morning, the blankets were a tangled heap around his ankles and his marriage was still unconsummated.

Hard work helped during the day, but even that was beginning to wear thin. Heaving the last bale onto the stack in the mow, Clayt climbed down the makeshift ladder to the main floor and almost stepped on one of Haley's cats. The cat yowled as if he'd done it on purpose. Looking at him strangely, Jason Tucker gave him a wide berth. Folks had been doing that a lot this past week. Clayt couldn't help it. He was getting next to no sleep and even less peace.

He was tired. He was edgy. He was agitated. He was a man, dammit. A married man.

This sleeping arrangement had to stop. He had a right to a little privacy with his own wife.

"Let's call it a day," he said to his red-haired hired hand.

Jason Tucker glanced from Clayt to the house and back again. "Whatever you say, boss."

That's right, Clayt thought as he walked through his own back door ten minutes later. He was the boss, which meant that he was in charge of the ranch. And he was Haley's father, which meant that he made the rules. Hanging his hat by the door, he knew what his first new rule was going to be.

All dogs and daughters would move to another room.

He made a pit stop in the bathroom to wash up. When he was finished, he heard voices coming from the other side of the house. Sidestepping the noisiest creaks in the floor, he followed the sound.

"I was only six years old when my parents drowned, but sometimes I can still hear my dad's deep voice and see his strong hands."

Clayt held perfectly still, listening to the quiet undertones in Mel's voice. He'd been twelve when Joe and Ellie McCully had drowned in the Bad River. He still remembered it in vivid detail. At the time he'd been more concerned about Wyatt than about Wyatt's little sister. Mel had always seemed so tough, so resilient. He still had both his parents, and as soon as his grandmother was well, they'd come back to the ranch where they'd always lived. Maybe talking to Mel, who'd lost both her parents at an early age, would help Haley come to terms with her mother's desertion.

Melody held perfectly still while Haley clipped a big

gaudy earring on her earlobe. "What about your mother?" Haley asked.

It wasn't easy to hold back a smile at the earnest expression in Haley's brown eyes. It had been Haley's idea to play beauty shop, and her hand had applied the red lipstick and rouge to both their faces.

"What do you remember about *her?*" Haley prodded.

"Well, let's see. She used to laugh a lot. Especially late at night when I was falling asleep."

"What did she look like?" Haley asked, pinning a lock of Melody's hair up with a bright red comb.

"Except for a few blurry snapshots, I barely remember what she looked like. My grandfather says that the first time my dad brought her home to meet him he thought she looked as if she'd been put together by a committee. She was kind of skinny and her mouth and eyes were too big for her face. But then she smiled, and something shifted inside his chest. After that, he says he changed the entire way he measured beauty."

Melody had a feeling that Haley was too young to understand about inner beauty, but when she said, "Do you still miss them? Your parents, I mean," Melody knew the girl wasn't too young to understand heartache.

"Yes, Haley, sometimes I still miss my dad's deep voice telling me that everything's going to be okay. I love my grandfather to pieces, but sometimes it would be nice to be able to talk to my mother about girl things." After a deliberate pause, she asked, "Do you miss your mother?"

The child shrugged her narrow shoulders. "Maybe, but your mom's dead, so she can't come back for you like my mama's gonna do for me. I know nobody believes she'll come back, but I don't care what they think. I don't care."

Melody was afraid to look at the child for fear that Haley would read the worry in her eyes. No matter what Haley said, she cared very, very much.

"What did you do at school today?"

Haley clipped the other earring to Melody's ear before replying. "Nothing."

"Nothing?"

"Well, nothing that wasn't boring. But I heard a good joke. What's black and white and red all over?"

"A newspaper," Clayt said, strolling into the room.

Haley looked up from her position on the edge of the bed, seemingly at ease with her father's sudden appearance in her room. "No, silly. A skunk with diaper rash." Jumping off the bed, she spun around and said, "Well, Clayton, how do I look?"

Clayt cupped his chin in his hand, deep in thought. He'd been trying to get Haley to open up to him for months. Mel had been here less than one week and his daughter was baring her soul. No matter what Haley said, she was vulnerable. Dang. He didn't see how he could kick her and the dog out of his room now.

She smiled at him and plopped backward on the bed. She and Mel were both wearing one of his shirts. Haley's reached midcalf, but Mel's stopped above her knees. Both their faces were thick with makeup. Strangely, Mel didn't look bad. For a second she reminded him of somebody, but he couldn't put his finger on who. Her lips were painted ruby red, her eyebrows penciled on, her lashes as black as coal. There was rouge on her cheeks and glitter on her eyelids. She should have looked fake and gaudy. Leave it to her to look striking and full of energy and ready to take on the world.

The world wasn't what he was thinking about taking on.

"You must be hungry," she said. "How about supper?"

"Supper?" A dozen thoughts had been playing through his mind, and not one of them had anything to do with supper.

Haley joined him in the doorway. "It's soup, Clayton.

Homemade beef and vegetable. I helped Melody make it. Come on, you're gonna love it.''

He allowed his daughter to lead him from the room. Aside from the little episode with General Custer, Haley really did seem to be doing better. Wasn't she the reason he'd married Mel in the first place? He wasn't proud of the fact that his first marriage had been a total disaster. He'd married Victoria for all the wrong reasons, and Haley was paying the price. This time he'd married a woman who would be good to his only child. He and Victoria had spent the first month of their married life between the sheets, and look where that had gotten him. This time he'd been married for six days and had yet to see his wife naked. Mel was nothing like Victoria, and that was the way he liked it. She was good with Haley. And he had to admit the soup smelled good. Trying not to focus on the sway of his wife's hips as she led the way to the kitchen, he told himself that three out of four wasn't bad.

''I believe this is the last of them,'' Louetta Graham said, placing a trayful of dirty dishes on the counter.

Melody glanced over her shoulder, the movement bringing the brightly wrapped package Lisa and Jillian had presented to her not more than fifteen minutes ago into her line of vision.

''Mind if I take a look?'' Louetta asked, motioning to the box.

Shaking her head, Melody turned around slowly just as Louetta pulled two filmy panties and matching bras out of the box. ''These are almost like mine.''

Melody noticed the red blotches tingeing Louetta's cheeks, but she couldn't help asking, ''Do you mean to tell me that you've purchased this kind of underwear?''

Staring at the toes of her sensible shoes, Louetta said, ''Not exactly.'' And then, as if she was sick and tired of being so painfully shy, she raised her chin and said, "Actually, Lisa gave them to me. Right after I stole them."

"Right after you what?" Melody asked.

"I didn't mean to," Louetta said hurriedly. "I saw all those pretty bits of lace and satin hanging on Lisa's clothesline and I thought I'd borrow them so I could hold them up to me in my room. I was just so tired of being plain and mousy, ya know? Anyway, I was putting the bras and panties back when Lisa discovered me. Wyatt was there, too. And Mother."

"What happened?" Melody asked, amazed.

Louetta's fingers shook slightly as she tucked an errant strand of hair back into her bun. "First of all, Mother almost fainted. I thought I was going to die. At the very least I expected to go to jail for stealing. Instead of pressing charges, Lisa gave the items to me as a gift. Isn't she amazing? Mother was so appreciative she invited Lisa to the next Ladies' Aid Society meeting. Isabell got her tail in a knot and said something to the effect of 'Over my dead body.' Mother didn't back down, and they haven't spoken since. I believe Mother did the right thing, but I know she misses Isabell terribly."

Melody lowered her dripping hands to her sides and shook her head. Wonders never ceased. "So that's what caused the rift between those two. For once the folks of Jasper Gulch didn't even come close to guessing the real reason for their silent feud."

Carefully placing the silky items back in the box, Louetta said, "Who would believe that I, plain old Louetta Graham, was capable of that?"

"Oh, Louetta. You and I are quite a pair, aren't we?"

"What do you mean?" Louetta asked shyly, starting to blush.

"We both grew up in a town chock-full of rugged cowboys, and we've both been overlooked by each and every one of them."

"But you're married to Clayt now."

Melody tipped her head and skewed her mouth to one side. "Can you keep a secret, Louetta? Of course you can. You've kept the reason for Isabell and Opal's feud to yourself for months. Clayt didn't marry me because he loves me. Don't get me wrong. He cares about me, and I think he respects me, but he married me because of Haley."

"At least you can say you're married."

"We're married, Louetta, but in name only."

"Do you mean that the two of you aren't, um, you know..." Louetta blushed the rest of the way.

"Sharing a bed?" Melody asked. "We're sharing a bed. But Haley shaved the dog, and now they're sleeping in the room with Clayt and me, and I'm here at the diner all day, and there just doesn't seem to be any time for, you know."

Keeping her gaze averted, Louetta said, "There's right now."

Melody did a double take. "You mean..."

The other woman nodded. Eventually she smiled. "I can handle things here in the diner for a few hours."

Melody stared at Louetta, tongue-tied. Up until now, she hadn't minded the fact that Haley and General Custer had been sleeping in the room with her and Clayt. She'd been hoping that he was coming to love her. There was no denying the fact that he *wanted* her. The problem was, she wanted him, too.

Something had started happening inside her more than a year ago. She'd grown tired of being lonely when the man she loved came into the diner three times a week. Clayt Carson had broken her heart dozens of times, but the night he'd stood up at a town meeting and proclaimed that Jasper Gulch needed more women, he'd nearly broken it for good. That was the day she'd realized that quiet hopelessness was getting her nowhere. Now she wasn't so sure waiting to make love with her husband was getting her anywhere, either.

She'd paid a visit to the library a few days ago. According to one renowned child psychologist, it was unhealthy to allow children to sleep with their parents. It was time to send Haley and the dog to another room. And it was time for her and Clayt to behave like a real married couple instead of just friends. She wanted Clayt to see her in a different light.

Did she really have the nerve to seduce her husband for the first time in broad daylight?

"I don't know," she said, covering her warm cheeks with her hands. "I wish I had a reason to go out to the ranch. I mean another reason."

The bell jingled over the door in the next room. Moments later Boomer Brown stuck his head in the kitchen. "Hey, Mel," the barrel-chested man said. "Since I was in Pierre this morning, I picked up this part for Clayt. Would you mind taking it to him when you go home tonight?"

Mel accepted the strange-looking gadget from Boomer's beefy hands. She didn't dare meet Louetta's eyes until Boomer had left. The second he was gone the two women burst out laughing. "Who says wishes don't come true?" Louetta asked.

Spinning on her heel, Melody headed for the door. Louetta's quiet voice slowed her steps. "Mel? I mean Melody? You might want to consider changing into these."

Melody accepted the box of bras and panties from Louetta's hand. Smoothing her fingers over the filmy lace and satin, she clamped her mouth shut and tamped down her nerves. Tucking the box beneath her arm, she took the stairs to her apartment. Although she couldn't quite bring herself to change into the filmy underclothes, she brushed her hair and dabbed a little perfume behind her ear. Without giving herself any time for second thoughts, she hurried back down the stairs. She said hello to the few folks she met on her way to her car, but she didn't stop to chat. After all, she had a husband to seduce. And a man's heart to capture once and for all.

Melody pulled into the driveway ten minutes later. She'd grown up on her grandfather's small spread south of town, so she knew the workings of a ranching operation. Men out here didn't work from nine to five. Their corner office was a stretch of land anywhere from two thousand to five thousand acres in size, which meant that Clayt could be anywhere.

She tried the big white house first. He'd been there sometime that morning because the phone book was out and the coffeepot was empty. But he wasn't there anymore.

Drying her sweaty palms on her jeans, she headed for the barn. The wind blew cold, the clouds churning up a storm on the horizon. Shivering, she pulled the lapels of her jacket together and poked her head inside the door. There were no lights on in the barn, and no sunbeams slanting through the windows.

A horse nickered, and Clayt appeared from the shadows. "Mel, what are you doing here? Is something wrong with Haley?"

Her heart lodged in her throat and her pulse jumped. The air whooshed out of her along with half her nerve. Clinging to the other half, she moseyed closer and said, "No. No, Clayt, Haley's in school. I'm sure she's fine. Where's Jason?"

Clayt heaved a saddle onto the rack and eyed Mel. Jason Tucker was one of the local boys who worked for him on the ranch. The boy was twenty years old and blushed almost as much as Louetta Graham did. Picking up a currycomb he walked back to Rambler and began grooming him.

He said, "I want to be ready to start roundup in a day or two. I sent Jason into Pierre for supplies. Did you come out here for anything special?"

Melody almost gulped. Her gaze caught on the movement of Clayt's hand as he smoothed it over Rambler's black coat. His skin was tanned, his knuckles large, the spread of his fingers wide. He was really very good with his hands. Those big, capable, strong hands.

"Mel?"

"Hmm?"

The currycomb stilled on Rambler's side. "Mind telling me what you're doing here in the middle of the afternoon?"

"Oh," she said, coming to her senses a little at a time. "Boomer dropped off a part he said you wanted, and I, um, left the diner in Louetta's care for the afternoon."

"You have the rest of the afternoon off?"

She nodded.

A hundred thoughts scrambled through Clayt's mind, but only one sensation took hold deep in his body. There was no sense pretending that he wasn't reacting to the expression in Mel's wide blue eyes. Suddenly he understood the reason for her uncharacteristic shyness. Damn, the woman was something else.

A need had been building in him all week, growing every time he crawled into bed next to her. Up until now he'd done a pretty darn good job of resisting her. Not that it hadn't cost him. He was a lot of things, stubborn and ornery, to name a few, but he was also honest, and he honestly didn't have an ounce of restraint left to his name.

He took a step closer. The horse nickered, the wind howled, and the first spattering of rain pelted the barn's metal roof.

"Mel," he said, and then, quieter, huskier, throatier, "Melody."

Chapter Eight

Melody brought her face up and slowly turned, her eyes meeting Clayt's in the weak autumn light. She felt a fast little jolt, followed by a softening sensation around her heart. "It's starting to pour outside."

"I know."

"We'll get soaked if we make a run for the house," she whispered as the water ran down the windowpanes.

His boot creaked as he shifted closer. "Then we'll have to wait the storm out in here."

"In here?"

"I can't think of a better way to spend a rainy afternoon, can you?"

Melody didn't think there was anything in the world softer than the gray of Clayt's eyes at that moment, or anything more masculine than the shape of his lips and the angle of his chin. She'd known him all her life, but she'd never realized what a unique combination of colors he was with his tanned skin and gray eyes and dark brown hair. His voice had been little more than a rasp in the semidarkness, but it made his intentions vibrantly clear.

His fingers filtered through her hair, moving to her shoulders, gliding down to her waist, only to work their way back up again where he opened the first button on her shirt. He kissed her before he'd unfastened the second button. By the time the kiss had ended, her shirt hung open, the cool air sending shivers along her exposed skin. His big hands encircled her waist, slowly inching up, bringing warmth where her shivers had been. He removed her coat then peeled the shirt from her body, and for a moment she wished she had taken the time to change into the pretty bra. The next thing she knew, her bra had joined her shirt and jacket on the floor, and Clayt was inhaling a ragged breath, releasing it on a moan the instant his palms covered her pale flesh.

Her breasts swelled beneath his hands, and she forgot all about being shy. This was her husband, the man she loved, the man she wanted to be her first lover. Her only lover.

Emboldened by her thoughts, she reached up and worked his buttons free. Her fingers were amazingly agile, the slight quiver more need than nerves. When his shirt landed on the straw behind her, he gathered her close as if he'd been waiting to experience the feel of man against woman for a long, long time.

The rest of their clothes came off in a tumble of boots, the clink of belt buckles and the rustle of denim. Completely naked, Clayt reached for a plaid blanket hanging over an empty stall. Spreading it over the new straw, he stretched out on his side, drawing her down with him. He kissed her, and when he felt her shudder, he kissed her again.

He wanted to go slow; he'd vowed to go slow, but as his hands glided over smooth skin and breasts ripe for his touch, all thoughts but one fled his mind. He caressed her, urging her to make a slow discovery with her own hands, her own lips, her own arms and legs and body. All the while his hands sought, his lips tantalized, his body strained. When she whimpered, letting him know that her need was as strong as his, he shifted his position and slowly joined them together.

He tried to be careful, but she moaned softly and opened her eyes, and he was lost. Her eyes looked violet in the gray light inside the barn, her skin pale ivory, her lips pink and swollen from his kisses. She smoothed her hands down his back, gliding them lower and lower.

"Mel." He sucked in a deep breath, his restraint slipping.

"Mmm," she whispered, moving against him.

"Easy, honey."

Instead of giving him a second to catch his breath, Melody raised her hips and moaned softly. She felt his restraint ebb out of him the way a wave receded from the shore. He grasped her by the hips, his eyes drifted closed, and a look unlike anything she'd ever seen crossed his face. He began to move, sending the most incredible sensations deep inside her body.

This was what she'd been waiting for all her adult life, this claiming of a man for his woman, a husband for his wife. It might have been sex between two consenting adults, but she believed it was more than that. It was an ultimate gift from one to the other, a gift that made everything in life seem sweeter and more worthwhile.

A long time later, after the soaring sensations all around her began to subside, his movements became less frenzied, and her heart swelled to bursting with love. Clayt had been even more incredible than she'd imagined, what he'd done to her, how he'd made her feel surpassing anything her fantasies could have conjured up.

He rolled to his side, the sound of the rain on the roof and the wind in the rafters finding its way into her consciousness once again. Feeling strong and pliant and oh, so womanly, she kissed his shoulder and said, "Not bad for a rookie, huh?"

Clayt felt a chuckle start low in his throat. "Mel," he said, running his hand from her shoulder to her hip and back again, "I'd call that a lot better than not bad."

She smiled and shivered, but she made no move to cover herself or to reach for her clothes. If he'd ever thought for a second that Mel McCully would have been this responsive, he would have taken a closer look at her a long time ago. But a man couldn't spend his entire life on a ranch without recognizing the importance of the right time and the right place and the right order. Out here the seasons blended, one following the other the way night followed day and rain followed drought and rebirth followed rain. What had happened between him and Mel might not have worked before. A few moments ago it had worked amazingly well.

He'd been a dreamer once. When he was young he couldn't see how gazing at the rolling hills in the distance could help but instill quiet in the hearts of men. He'd known early on that Luke didn't feel the way he did about the land. Wyatt didn't, either, for that matter. One had become the best vet in this part of South Dakota, the other an extremely kind-hearted and shrewd sheriff. Only Clayt had continued the tradition his great-great-grandfather had started more than a hundred years ago.

He'd questioned his choices these past few years. Loneliness tended to have that effect on even the most steadfast of men. His first marriage had ended badly. He'd still been a dreamer back then. Now he was much more rooted in reality. This time he'd married for different reasons. This time there were no stars in his eyes.

He settled back into the straw, listening to the rain pelt the roof and the wind rattle the windows. The downpour was going to wreak havoc with the roundup, but he had to admit that it was going to be nice to have a warm house to come home to. A warm woman, too.

Melody glanced up and found Clayt looking at her. Her breath caught just below the hollow in her throat. There was a slight tenderness in her lower body, and although she had no other point of reference, making love had been amazingly sweet and poignant. She felt the tiniest bit weepy, and knew of only one thing that would make everything that had happened even more perfect. Her heart had never held so much love for one person. She yearned to tell Clayt, and she ached to hear him utter words of love in return.

"What are you thinking about?" she asked, feeling strangely shy now that her passion had been spent.

Clayt shrugged and slowly sat up. "Oh," he said, "I don't know. The rain, I guess, and the roundup. And you."

Her heart skipped a beat and her hopes soared. Could this be the moment she'd been waiting for? The moment when he told her he loved her?

He glanced at her, his gaze dropping by degrees. When it became apparent that he wasn't going to say any more, she reached for the article of clothing closest to her and quickly shimmied into her plain cotton panties. Since her bra was nowhere in sight, she pulled on her jeans, hopped to her feet and reached for her shirt. When she was covered, she said, "What, *exactly*, were you thinking about me?"

His belt buckle clinked as he fastened his jeans, his shirt rustling as he tucked it in. "I was just thinking that you'd probably like to bring the rest of your things out here. This is your home now. Any changes you want to make, well, feel free."

She leaned down to tug on one boot, thankful to have a reason to avert her gaze. This wasn't exactly what she'd been waiting all her life to hear. "What do you mean?" she asked.

"If you like your sofa better than mine, we'll haul yours in and mine out. I'm not going to be much help until after the roundup is finished, but we can move all your things into the house when that's over. Shoot, you might as well rent your place out. The extra income might come in handy."

Melody's hopes thudded at the same time the boot she'd been gripping fell to the floor. That was it? She'd just made love for the first time in her life, and all Clayt could think about was added income?

She looked away, out the window at the rain and the gray sky. "That won't be necessary, Clayt."

"I know, but it's no trouble," he said, oblivious to the change in the tone of her voice.

"It won't be any trouble because I'm not going to move all my things out to the ranch."

"What do you mean?"

At least she finally had his attention. "I'll bring what I want, what I'll use, but I'll leave the rest there."

He rubbed his chin as if he didn't fully understand what she was saying. "Do you want to rent the apartment furnished?"

"I'm not going to rent the apartment."

"You're not."

"No, I'm not."

Clayt heard a dull ringing in ears. He recognized the sound as one he always heard moments before his temper went through the roof. Narrowing his eyes, he stared at Mel, trying to figure out who she reminded him of. It had happened before. Then, like now, he couldn't put his finger on who it was. Telling himself to be patient—no minor feat for a Carson—he said, "You're my wife. You live here now. For crying out loud, it isn't as if I'm trying to take your rent money. It would be yours. Geez, Mel, I thought you'd appreciate the extra cash."

Her chin came up in a manner that could only mean trouble. "So what you're saying is that I shouldn't look a gift horse in the mouth."

The ringing in his ears turned into a deafening silence. Hell, that wasn't what he'd said at all. He half expected her to stomp her foot and storm out. Instead, she raised her violet eyes to his and quietly said, "In case you haven't noticed, I'm not a horse."

She turned, retrieving her jacket from a pile of loose straw. All grace and affronted dignity, she strode out of the barn and into the pouring rain. A sense of déjà vu washed over Clayt. Victoria used to walk away from an argument the same way.

He went perfectly still. This wasn't the first time Mel had reminded him of someone else. But it was the first time he'd figured out who.

Marrying Victoria had been the biggest mistake of his life. The only good thing that had come out of the entire union was Haley. He'd done everything in his power to make Victoria happy. In return, she'd stomped on his heart and spit out his pride. She'd insisted upon keeping her apartment in Pierre, too. And she'd run back there every time she'd decreed that he spent too much time on the range. He could still see the way she wrinkled up her nose because he smelled of horse and dust and sweat, and he vividly recalled the way she'd let every gossip in town know exactly where she was going and why.

He scooped his hat out of the straw, his eyes catching on a scrap of material underneath it. He folded his fingers around the plain white bra, desire tugging at his insides all over again.

The memory of how Mel had kissed him and touched him washed over him. He had to be mistaken. Mel wasn't like Victoria at all. She certainly hadn't wrinkled up her nose a little while ago. Hell, they'd made love in a barn that smelled of horses and hay. She'd been ardent and passionate and so darn responsive she'd practically come apart in his arms.

He wouldn't have expected the old Mel to do that. But then, he wouldn't have expected the old Mel to keep her apartment, either. *Melody* was another story.

The old Mel was nothing like Victoria, but he wasn't so sure about this new creature who called herself Melody. Whether she planned to stomp on his pride or not, the fact that she was keeping her apartment led him to believe that she was keeping her options open. They hadn't discussed this. They hadn't discussed anything. For all he knew, she could be planning to move back there one day soon.

He glanced into the shadows where the blanket was still spread out on the straw. What had just happened between them had been incredible. Sex usually was. But a roll in the hay did not a marriage make. He happened to know it took a lot more than that. It took commitment. That was one thing Victoria had been sorely lacking. Now he wasn't so sure about Mel.

He'd seen how good she was with Haley. For his daughter's sake as well as for his own, he had to find out what Mel's plans were. Making a fist around the bra, he crammed his hat on his head and followed the course she'd taken into the house.

He was soaked by the time he set foot inside the back door. Mel, who was drying her hair with a towel, turned to face him. Her eyes looked wet and luminous; for a moment he thought she might have been crying. But then she bristled, and he realized it must have been the rain.

Hanging his hat by the door, he said, "Mel, we have to talk."

Melody took a shuddering breath and straightened her spine. *See?* she told herself. Everything was going to be all right. She'd overreacted in the barn, that's all. It was perfectly understandable. She'd just made love for the first time. Her emotions were bound to be close to the surface. Clayt must have realized that, too, and was here to set things right. Swallowing the lump in her throat, she said, "What did you want to talk about?"

"You're my wife."

"Yes?"

"As my wife, I insist that you give up your apartment."

She felt her eyes narrow and her lips thin. "Oh, you do?"

Opening his hand, he stared at what appeared to be her bra. He seemed to lose his bearings for a few seconds, a muscle working in his throat, a pained expression crossing his face. "I demand it, dammit. You live here now. With Haley and me. And we have no need for the apartment."

Melody fought valiantly to hold on to her temper. "What if I want to keep it?"

He took a step. Holding out his hand, he dropped the bra on the kitchen table. "You are one contrary woman, do you know that?"

"And you're one stubborn man."

"Tell me something I don't already know."

I love you, whispered through her mind. But she didn't say it out loud. He already knew that. He had for years.

Folding her arms and raising her chin, she said, "I'm not giving up my apartment, Clayt. Maybe I should go back there tonight."

She didn't know what to make of the backward step he took or the way he clamped his mouth shut as if he'd just taken a fist in the jaw. Melody had a bad feeling about this. She wanted a beautiful love affair with her husband. She was beginning to worry that she going to get a bad ending and a broken heart.

"Let me know what you decide," he said, a stony expression on his face. "I'll have to make arrangements for Haley."

He reached for his hat, turned on his heel and left. The glass in the door didn't rattle in his wake, but the door closed with a click that was just as ominous as any slam.

Melody lifted the delicate satin from the old trunk. Holding the dress against her body, she smoothed her hand over the narrow waistline and down the full skirt. The sleeves were long, the satin yellowed with age. It was still the most beautiful gown Melody had ever seen. It had been her mother's, and she'd always dreamed of wearing it, too.

She'd had to give up that dream when she'd married Clayt before the justice of the peace. Now, she was trying to decide whether to take the gown to the ranch with the rest of her clothes, or leave it here in her apartment. Staring at her reflection, she moved as if in slow motion. There was no place in her life or in her dreams for her mother's wedding gown anymore. Draping the beautiful dress over the foot of the bed, she went back to her earlier task.

The closet in her apartment was almost empty, her dresser top completely cleared off. As far as she could tell, she had everything she needed. No matter what she'd told Clayt earlier, she didn't want to stay here tonight. She wanted to be with him. And she wanted to have a real marriage.

Although Louetta would never come right out and ask, her eyes had been full of questions when Melody had arrived back at the diner in time for the supper crowd. Melody had done her best to put on a happy face. If Louetta had seen through her facade, she hadn't let on. As Melody had served supper to folks she'd known all her life, she'd thought long and hard about what had happened between her and Clayt.

His anger didn't make sense. *She* was the one who'd

taken it upon herself to consummate their marriage. She hadn't expected candlelight or flowers, and she hadn't gotten it. Terms of endearment and words of love would have been nice, but she hadn't gotten any of those, either. What she'd gotten for her trouble was incredible sex and then a cold shoulder. She'd always known Clayt was old-fashioned. She understood his desire to support his family. It was what men out here did. He'd acted as if her decision to keep her apartment was a personal assault on his manhood. If he wasn't so thickheaded he would have realized that all he had to do to keep her was to love her. It was all he'd ever had to do.

What he didn't seem to understand was that she *couldn't* give up her apartment. If she did, and he never fell in love with her, she would have no place to go. She hoped she never had to sleep in her apartment again. After all, she wanted a real marriage, one based on respect and passion and especially on love.

She carted the boxes to the door. By the time she'd made her fourth trip out to her car, she'd come to another realization. Clayt Carson was as stubborn as he was tall, but when it came to pride, the two of them could go nose to nose. She'd loved him from afar for years. Today they'd come as close as two people could be. Her body had reacted with the most delicious sensations every time she'd thought about it since. Clayt had been a wonderful lover. Not that she was surprised. He was a strong, good man. Now that they'd been intimate, she was even more certain that a real marriage was worth fighting for.

Smiling to herself as she loaded the last box into her trunk, she swiped her hands together and thought about the coming evening. Clayt had married her because of Haley. Melody could live with that reason, as long as it didn't remain the only reason.

Haley was doing well. The girl had a quick mind and an

uncanny sense of humor. She was amazingly hardworking and didn't seem to mind washing dishes to earn her pay. Of course the girl was special. She was a Carson, after all. She was laughing more and looking less forlorn every day. It was time she moved back into her own room. Even the psychologist who'd written that book agreed. Once Haley was settled back in her own bed, safe and secure, Melody would be able to entice her husband to love her, despite his ornery, stubborn ways. Because Clayt Carson wasn't the least bit stubborn or ornery when he was making love. Smiling to herself, she thought it was highly possible that *that* was when his heart would be the most open to love.

She pointed her car toward the Carson ranch, certain that she was on the right track where their marriage was concerned. She was going to need a little privacy to carry out her plan, but she should be able to accomplish that. With her resolve sitting like a rock inside her, she pulled into the driveway of the house she would call home just as soon as Clayt came to love her.

"Clayt, your timing's perfect."

Clayt stopped just inside the door. It was ten o'clock. Although Mel had called hours ago to let him know that she wouldn't be staying at her place and would be able to watch Haley after all, he hadn't been entirely certain what he'd find when he finally came inside tonight. One thing he hadn't expected was her warm smile. Suddenly feeling as if he was on uneven footing, he took another step into the room. "Perfect?" he asked. "Perfect for what?"

She turned lithely, folding a towel over the sink. "Perfect for my surprise. Are you hungry?"

He shook his head. "I came up to the house earlier and had a bite to eat before you and Haley got home. Where is Haley, anyway?"

She smiled again, causing his breath to get stuck in his

throat. "When I checked on her a little while ago, she was sound asleep upstairs."

Feeling confused and disoriented, Clayt said, "Haley's upstairs?"

She nodded, slowly moving backward. "That's part of the surprise."

Clayt hadn't realized he'd followed until he found himself in his bedroom. Glancing around, he said, "Where's the General?"

"That's the second part of my surprise."

He heard a faint rustle of material. Turning, he took a deep breath and drew the scent of jasmine to the bottom of his lungs. "Mel, what are you doing?"

As one second followed another, her expression changed in the most subtle of ways. She raised her lips and lifted her eyes to his. "Something tells me that in a moment or two you'll figure that out for yourself."

Clayt didn't see how he would be able to figure anything out as long as Mel kept looking at him like that. Her hair was fastened in a whimsical knot on top of her head, wispy tendrils cascading onto her forehead and over her ears and along the collar of her shirt. That was a shirt she was wearing, wasn't it? It was styled like a shirt, with buttons and long sleeves, but he'd never seen a shirt in that thin, shiny fabric. He could easily make out the gentle slope of her breasts and the delicate ridge of her collarbone. The shirt barely brushed the middle of her thighs—her bare thighs— the material shimmering over her legs with every movement she made.

While his heart chugged to life and his breathing jumpstarted, his gaze did a slow climb back up her body, only to get caught on her lips all over again. Without conscious thought, he reached out his hand and traced those pink, full, wet lips with his finger.

Turning her luminous blue eyes on him, she said, "What do you think of my surprise so far?"

He almost didn't answer. He almost couldn't. But he happened to glance at the rug where General Custer had been spread out these past several days, and then at the foot of the bed where Haley had curled into a ball every night, and he found himself saying, "How did you manage to convince Haley to move back to her own room?"

"I didn't. I convinced General Custer to move upstairs. Haley followed. Is that all right with you?"

His mouth had gone so dry he couldn't have spoken if his life depended upon it. Mel's skin looked smooth, her hair soft, her lips utterly appealing. The light was turned low, the covers were turned back. Glancing at the boxes stacked in the corner, he felt as if he was standing on the bottom of the ocean, his body expanding despite the pressure pushing against it. He and Mel had made love that very afternoon. There was no reason for this need to be back in full force. And yet it was.

"You said yourself that you have a busy day ahead of you," she said, steadily moving closer. "Don't you think we should turn in, too?"

In a daze, he eyed his big bed. And then Mel. And then the boxes she'd placed her things in when she'd brought them from her apartment—her apartment, which she insisted upon keeping despite the fact that they were now married. "Did you change your mind about leasing your apartment?" he asked quietly.

Melody's heart skipped a beat. This was where she'd planned to tell Clayt that she wanted a real marriage, one based on mutual respect and desire, on dignity and on love. With her heart swelling and her thoughts turning hazy and warm, she said, "You, Clayt Carson, are a complex man, and if I live to be a hundred, I doubt I'll ever completely understand you, but..."

Her voice trailed away because he was looking at her with that sleepy glint in his eyes that didn't necessarily mean he was sleepy. He placed his hand on her shoulder, slowly letting it glide to her elbow. Closing her eyes, she concentrated on the warmth of his palm and the strength in those long fingers stroking her arm.

"You were saying?" he asked.

She'd had the evening all planned. She'd scented her bathwater and she'd chosen this nightshirt, hoping she could entice her husband into bed and lure him into love. Placing her hand over his, she willed him to see the depth of her feelings for him. "I have no intention of stomping on your pride, Clayt."

Clayt waited for a but. The fact that she hadn't uttered it didn't mean there wasn't one. "You have no intention of stomping on my pride, *but* you're not giving up your apartment. Is that right?"

"I didn't stay there tonight, Clayt. I'm here because I want to be, because I want this marriage to work, because..."

Glancing around the room where the lamp was turned to its lowest setting and the blankets were folded back invitingly, he almost forgot everything except the desire pooling low in his body. The same thing had happened often enough back when he'd been married to Victoria. The thought of Victoria brought back his last ounce of sanity and self-preservation and allowed him to take a backward step.

"Clayt, what's wrong?"

He swallowed the need that was jamming up his vocal chords and said, "You're tired. You've obviously had a long day, what with the diner and unpacking and taking care of Haley. Maybe you should get some sleep. I still have some things to do out in the barn and in the shed to get ready for the roundup tomorrow. Don't wait up.'' He swung around and headed out the door.

The wind blew through his coat, and the first spattering of snow pelted his face and hands. It wasn't unheard of for it to start snowing in October in this part of South Dakota, but he hoped the heavy stuff held off for as long as possible. If they were lucky and the weather held and the herd stayed together, they'd make it through the winter with a minimum of losses.

Reaching for the engine part Boomer had picked up in Pierre that very afternoon, he opened the hood of the Jeep he used out on the range. The roundup would be underway bright and early tomorrow morning. A few days from now a good share of the calves would be shipped to feeder farms farther east. He'd already spent days preparing for it, but the work was far from done. He told himself to concentrate on the work and not on the woman who was probably curled up in his bed right now. It would have been a lot easier to do if he could just get the memory of the way Mel had felt in his arms that very afternoon out of his mind. No matter how hard he tried, he couldn't seem to forget the way her hair had looked spread out on that plaid blanket or the way her sighs had blended with the rain on the roof.

If Mel McCully, the contrary, ill-tempered woman had been difficult to get out of his mind, it was nothing compared to the trouble he was having keeping Melody Carson, his softly alluring wife out of his thoughts. His pride was the only thing that kept him from striding back into the house and taking up where they'd left off—his pride and the fact that he wasn't so sure he knew who Melody Carson was.

Oh, he'd known her well enough when she'd been his best friend's plain kid sister. Her transition into womanhood hadn't been particularly noteworthy. She'd gone from wielding a broom in her grandfather's kitchen to wielding a broom in her own diner. She'd always been skinny. Technically, he supposed she still was. But the braid she'd always worn was gone, and honestly, there was nothing plain about her anymore.

He was a man, and he certainly didn't mind the subtle changes in her appearance. What he minded were the similarities to Victoria. He'd been blinded by *her* beauty a long time ago. He'd never been proud of the fact that he hadn't made an intelligent choice in asking her to marry him. He'd thought Mel was different. Now he didn't know what to think.

Doing what he always did when his life was a mess and the weather was worse and only backbreaking, long hours kept his head above water, he dug in his heels and reefed on the wrench. His fingers got greasy and his knuckles got skinned, but he didn't care. Tearing apart the engine didn't quite allow him to forget the invitation in Mel's eyes, but at least it kept him occupied long into the night.

Chapter Nine

Melody threw the covers off and swung her feet over the side of the bed. She'd been staring at the ceiling for more than two hours and enough was enough. She was going to march out to that shed and force Clayt to talk to her. "Listen, you," she would say, "I went to a lot of trouble to seduce you tonight. The least you can do is cooperate."

She made it as far as the back door before her smarting ego stopped her in her tracks. No matter how much she wanted to give him a piece of her mind, she didn't think she could handle two rejections in one night. Retracing her steps, she climbed back into bed and pulled the covers up to her chin.

She didn't pretend to know a lot about the male half of the species, and she knew even less about sex. But Clayt had wanted her tonight, at least physically. The strain of desire had been evident on his face, in the set of his shoulders and in the depth of his voice. Yet he'd denied himself, thereby denying her at the same time. If she'd had more experience with this sort of thing it might not have hurt so bad. If she'd had more experience, she might know what to do.

Hearing the back door open, she tiptoed out of the bedroom, stopping in the archway between the kitchen and living room. Clayt was filling a glass with tap water when he noticed her. He lowered the glass and took a sharp breath, but made no move to lessen the distance between them.

The yellow light over the old enamel sink accented the shadows under his eyes. She wanted to ask if he would mind explaining what went on in the deepest recesses of a man's mind. While he was at it he could tell her what he wanted from this marriage. With the cold seeping into her bare feet and her confidence ebbing, she found herself asking some obscure question about the ranch and the roundup.

He eyed her cautiously and answered just as obscurely before lowering his glass of water to the counter behind him. "I didn't mean to wake you," he said quietly.

With silence stretching taut between them, she skirted the table and grasped the back of a chair. "I must have been pretty bad out in the barn today."

She couldn't be sure who was more surprised by her outburst, but staring at him in the ensuing silence, she knew he couldn't have been more mortified than she was.

"You weren't bad at all," he finally said. "*You* were there, Mel. You have to know how much I enjoyed it."

She took a deep breath before moving to the next chair. "This is my first marriage. I don't have the wisdom of experience like you do. What am I supposed to do here? What do you *want* me to do?"

A muscle worked in his jaw, and his eyes thinned into a narrow squint. "I want you to be yourself."

She rounded the table without thinking, because all her thoughts were tied up with what he'd said. Spreading her hands wide, she asked, "Who else would I be?"

"That's a good question."

She sputtered, baffled. "Of course it's a good question. That's why I asked it."

"Look," he said, running a hand through his hair. "It's late, and we both have to be up early. What do you say we call it a day?"

That was it? He'd turned down her advances, then kept her lying awake half the night while he fiddled around with some engine part in the shed, and when he finally came inside, he told her he wanted her to be herself, and then, when she was smack dab in the middle of trying to figure him out, he thought they should call it a day?

"Hold it right there, buster."

Clayt had barely made it to the doorway before Mel's sharp voice stopped him in his tracks. He could practically see the sparks in her eyes. Her hands were on her hips, her shoulders raised in defiance, her feet planted firmly on the floor. That stance used to irritate the hell out of him. Tonight it eased the tension from his muscles and made him feel like grinning.

"What's so funny?"

"I'm not laughing at you," he said, turning to face her. "I just had a flashback, that's all."

"A flashback?"

His nod was barely discernible, his steps toward her slow and steady. "I was thinking about that time when Wyatt and I caught you trying out your grandfather's chew in the hayloft. You couldn't have been much more than ten years old. If I remember right you were wearing a nightshirt then, too. Ooo-eee, were you mad. You planted your hands on your hips and raised your chin at that haughty angle you do and let us have it. You always did have a sharp tongue, Mel. Although I didn't realize it until lately, it's one of the things I like about you."

Melody's hands slid down her hips. When they were

hanging limply at her sides, she closed her gaping mouth, but there wasn't much she could do about her dumbfounded stare. Clayt's jaw was nearly black with whisker stubble, his hair in need of a trim, his clothes windblown. She couldn't look at him without remembering how his hair had felt beneath her fingertips earlier that afternoon, and how the sandpaper stubble on his chin had rasped against her bare skin. Something was wrong with this picture. While she was remembering the sound and feel of making love, *he* was recalling one of the most embarrassing incidents of her life.

"Mel."

The closer he strode the more she had to raise her head to hold his gaze. He loomed over her, and she didn't like it, especially when he looked as if he had everything under control and she had no idea what was going on. Bristling, she said, "You're too tall to talk to, Clayt Carson."

He only smiled. "See? That's exactly what I expected you to say. This is what I meant. You don't have to try to be someone you're not."

"I don't."

"Not for me, you don't. We already know each other inside and out. I know you went to a lot of trouble earlier to surprise me, but I married you so there would be no surprises. I appreciate everything you've done for Haley, and I'd like a chance to do something for you in return."

"Gee, Clayt, that sounded almost as romantic as a handshake."

"That's what I'm getting at. The Mel I've always known wouldn't expect romance. Come on, Mel. We know each other's stories, and we know how to handle each other's tempers. You were the one who reminded me that we got married for Haley's sake. As far as I'm concerned, what happened in the barn is proof that we can make this work."

"Really?"

Although he nodded, she felt confused and disappointed.

"I'm going to be busy with the roundup these next few days, but maybe when it's over we could go out or something."

Melody didn't think there was much she could do except shrug. When Clayt reminded her that they could both use a little sleep, she crawled back into bed. After a quick shower, he came to bed, too. He seemed much more cool, calm and collected than he had earlier. Within minutes, his breathing was deep and even.

The sturdy old house withstood the onslaught of the relentless wind blowing across the plains. A cow lowed and a branch scraped the siding. Listening to the sounds of night, Melody tried to understand what had happened to her carefully laid plans. Somehow her relationship with Clayt had taken a giant step backward. For the life of her she didn't know what to do about it.

Clayt pushed the heavy barn door shut. Waving to his brother, Luke, and to Jason Tucker whose tires churned up loose gravel as he sped toward his warm house in town, Clayt pulled the brim of his hat lower on his forehead and glanced at the dark sky.

It was only nine o'clock. The soreness in his muscles made it seem a lot later. As of that moment the roundup was officially over and a good share of the calves born this year were on their way to feeder farms in Iowa. It was the first roundup he'd handled without his father at his side. Clayt was cold and tired to the bone, but he was proud of a job well done.

Scraping the mud and grime from his boots, he headed for the house. The porch light reached out to him, but it was the sight of Haley and Mel on the other side of the lighted window that lengthened his stride. Their heads were bent close at the table, the light casting a pale glow over both of them. An entirely different feeling of pride washed over him. Things had gotten off to a rocky start between him and Mel, but little by little he hoped they would get back to normal. He would tease, she would bristle. He would grin, she would fume. Through it all she would be the Mel he'd always known.

As usual, the low drone of the television carried to his ears the instant he opened the door. Haley looked up, a light in her eyes and a smile on her face. He was cold and tired, but the warmth in his kitchen and the happiness on Haley's face was well worth the discomfort.

"Know what you call a sleeping bull?" she asked, meeting him at the door.

Rubbing his chin thoughtfully, he said, "Steak?"

"No, silly, a bulldozer."

Clayt left his boots on the rug and his hat and coat on the pegs by the door and smiled at Mel over the top of Haley's light brown hair. Mel averted her gaze. She'd been doing that a lot these past two days. He'd hurt her feelings when he'd turned down her advances a few nights ago. At the time he'd been worried that history was repeating itself. Now he was pretty sure that wasn't going to happen.

Although he still didn't see any reason for Mel to keep her apartment in town, he realized he shouldn't have been surprised that she'd done it. Her stubborn streak was one of the things that made her who she was. The six-and-a-half-year difference in their ages had never fazed her, and while she might claim that he was too tall to talk to, she'd never let his height intimidate her. He liked that about her. There were a lot of things he liked about her.

The smell of leftovers wafted from the warm oven. It had been hours since he'd eaten, but Clayt was more aware of another hunger deep inside him. Glancing at the clock on the stove, he said, "It's bedtime, Haley."

For a moment Haley looked surprised and then belligerent. She started to protest like she always did, but she glanced at Mel and her whole demeanor changed. The next thing he knew Haley was striding toward the stairs. Sounding older than her nine years, she said, "I hafta get to bed if I'm gonna keep up my grades *and* hold down a job. Night, Melody. Night, Dad."

Dad?

Clayt must have answered, but he couldn't seem to drag his eyes from Haley's back. This was the first time she'd called him anything except Clayton in years. Watching as she practically floated up the stairs, he said, "There's no doubt that she's doing better, Mel. And there's no doubt that you're a big part of the reason." He turned around slowly. "Have I thanked you lately?"

Melody's hands stilled on the magic markers she'd been gathering on the table, a force bigger than her slowly drawing her gaze. Clayt had been up before dawn yesterday and had come inside long after she'd gone to bed, only to start the process all over today. He'd spent the past two days in a saddle and had no business looking so good. He had no business making her heart speed up, either.

One of these days he was going to have to break down and get a haircut. Sooner or later he was going to have to stop staring at her mouth. Eventually she would have to remember that she was mad at him.

He turned suddenly, heading for the stairs.

"Where are you going?" she called.

He glanced over his shoulder. "I thought I'd go upstairs and tell Haley good-night."

She waited until he was gone to put her elbows on the table and lower her face into her hands. She did *not* understand him, and it wasn't from lack of trying. She could have sworn he'd wanted her moments ago. Of course, she'd been convinced he'd wanted her two nights ago, too. Both times he'd completely surprised her by walking away.

Slowly lowering her hands from her face, she glanced from the oven where his supper was warming to the open stairway in the next room. If Haley was in her usual form, Melody would have a long time to continue thinking about it, because that child loved to talk long into the night.

Leaving the markers and the glue Haley had used earlier on the table, Melody strode into the bathroom. Balancing on the edge of the old claw-footed tub, she started the water. She added scented oil, peeled off her clothes and sank into the hot water, lost in thought.

A long time ago she'd wished that Clayt would marry her. Now she wished she had also thought to ask that he love her. She'd been so sure she was on the right track where he was concerned, so certain that she'd find the way to his heart while they were making love. They'd made love. If anything, she understood him less now than she ever had.

She washed her face and scrubbed every inch of her body. After pulling the plug, she dried herself with one of the towels she'd brought from her place, thinking all the while. She was afraid it was hopeless. Maybe Clayt didn't like skinny women. Maybe things would have been different if she had more experience. Maybe her instincts were all wrong and her—

The door opened, and her thoughts trailed away. Clayt stood perfectly still in the doorway. His chest was bare, his jeans slung low on his hips. His belt was missing, the button closure on his jeans unfastened. He had a washboard stomach, a broad chest and a face that had always been shaped by strong lines and masculine hollows. Tonight his eyes were the darkest shade of gray she'd ever seen.

She couldn't move. When he reached his hand out, his fingers working the edges of her towel free, she couldn't even breathe. With a flick of his wrist, the ends parted and the towel slid to the floor.

"I'd like to make up for the other night," he said, his voice little more than a husky rasp in the steamy room.

His hand moved to her chest, pausing for a moment over her heart before inching its way to her breast. "Would you let me do that, Mel?" he whispered, his fingers squeezing and kneading.

"What if Haley comes downstairs?" she whispered.

He kicked the door shut with one foot. And then he was kissing her and touching her and molding her to his lean body. She didn't know how she'd gone from standing to lying on her back on the rug. She only knew that Clayt had joined her in the confining space between the sink and the bathtub, and that his hands were doing the most amazing things, and her body was reacting in the most amazing way.

When she was certain she couldn't stand another second of his kisses and his touches and his caresses, he made them one. The pleasure was pure and explosive, and although it was over more quickly than the last time, it was no less intense. If anything she responded more completely, more profoundly, more instinctively than before.

Later she was curled on her side beneath the covers in bed. Her eyes drifted closed, Clayt's arm a welcome weight across her waist. "Night, Mel," he said close to her ear.

She felt warm and sated, but there was still something she wanted to understand. "Clayt?" she whispered in the darkness.

"Hmm?"

"Why do you still call me Mel?"

"That's your name."

The mattress was soft, the blankets blessedly warm. Wanting to understand before sleep gently claimed her, she whispered, "Everybody else calls me Melody. You're the only person who still calls me Mel. Why?"

His voice, when it came, was little more than a husky rasp in the darkness and seemed to come from far, far away.

"Because to me," he murmured, "Mel is who you'll always be."

Melody opened her eyes.

The room was dark, but as the events of the past few weeks played through her mind everything that had been hazy came into focus.

Because to me, Clayt had said, *Mel is who you'll always be.*

Mel. Not Melody.

Mel, Wyatt's little sister, Cletus McCully's granddaughter.

As the minutes ticked by, she faced the undeniable and dreadful truth. Clayt had asked *Mel* to marry him. Not because he loved her. But because he didn't.

She wanted to cry, but no tears came. She wanted to tell herself she was wrong, but she'd never been very good at lying. No wonder she hadn't felt any closer to Clayt after they'd made love. Making love hadn't changed anything, because Clayt didn't want anything to change. He'd fought his desire two nights ago, denying his need. A weaker man might have crumbled. A weaker man might have surrendered everything as long as he could satisfy his desire.

Clayt Carson wasn't a weaker man.

He was strong and stubborn. He was also the kind of hardworking, rugged man women used to travel thousands of miles to marry a hundred years ago. A handful of women had done the same thing much more recently. Once upon a time a woman might have settled for a loveless marriage. Melody couldn't do that. She had to find a way to show Clayt that he didn't have to settle, either.

But how? How did a woman go about showing a man who made his living by braving the elements, a man who had learned to ignore discomfort, a man who made decisions based on past experience and calculated risks that she was worth the risk to his heart?

* * *

If there was a way, Melody still hadn't discovered it two months later. A few things *had* changed, but others had stayed the same. Opal and Isabell still weren't speaking, and the local gossips were hungry for information. Louetta hadn't breathed a word to anybody else, but she had taken over all the duties involved with feeding the supper crowd. Some of the local boys had complained at first, but once they'd tasted Louetta's cooking, they'd shut up and ordered seconds.

The folks of Jasper Gulch were always on the lookout for a reason to throw a party. Lisa, Jillian and DoraLee were huddled at a table making plans for DoraLee and Boomer's engagement party right now. Now that Clayt's grandmother had nearly fully recovered from the stroke she'd had months ago, Hugh and Rita Carson were scheduled to return to the ranch soon. Melody liked Clayt's parents, but she felt as if her chance to have a real marriage was growing more slim with every passing day.

Not that she wasn't trying. Now that she had her evenings free, she spent more time with Clayt and Haley. In many ways it was nice. Haley seemed happy, and there had been times when Melody could almost believe that the moments of argument and humor, desire and affection that she and Clayt shared might one day lead to love. More often than not they led to a closed bedroom door and tangled sheets. He was always thoughtful, and very passionate. Sometimes, when he touched her just so, or murmured her name moments before sending her to the brink of the most incredible desire she'd ever imagined, she could almost believe he loved her. But when it was over and he was asleep, she would lie awake, staring at the ceiling, more lonely than she'd ever been in her life.

Filling a clean coffee carafe, Melody shook her head to clear it and trudged over to the table where DoraLee, Jillian and Lisa were sitting. "Need a refill?" she asked.

Three pairs of eyes raised to hers, and three women drew collective gasps. "You look done in," Lisa declared.

"Exhausted," Jillian added.

"Here, sugar, have a seat."

Melody sank into a chair.

"Is everything all right?" Jillian asked, pushing her red hair behind her shoulders.

"Did you and Clayt have an argument?" Lisa added.

"Clayt and Melody have always argued," DoraLee declared. "Isn't that right, sugar?"

Propping her chin in her hand, Melody said, "Actually, we've only had one major argument."

"It must have been a doozy to make you look this tired," Lisa said, her brown eyes soft and caring.

Melody didn't have the heart to tell her friends that quiet hopelessness was the real reason she felt so exhausted these days. Placing the coffee carafe in the middle of the table, she fiddled with the plain gold wedding band on her left hand. "I've known Clayt all my life, but I hardly understand him at all."

"I don't think women are supposed to understand men," DoraLee said, her round face looking younger since she'd fallen in love with Boomer.

"Do you want to tell us what you argued about?" Lisa asked.

Casting her three closest friends a tremulous smile, Melody said, "It happened weeks ago, and I'm not exactly sure how it started, but he told me I was contrary and I said something about looking a gift horse in the mouth and he demanded that I start leasing my apartment and I told him I was keeping it. Things went a little haywire after that. He said stuff and I said stuff and then he brought up my apartment again, and I said I might want to go back there some time."

"Oh, sugar, you didn't."

Melody looked at DoraLee, but all she could do was nod.

Smoothing a hand over her bleached blond hair, DoraLee said, "You might as well put on your high heels and stomp on his pride in the middle of Main Street."

Melody was getting a bad feeling about this. "What do you mean?"

"Don't you remember?" DoraLee asked. "Victoria used to run off to her apartment in Pierre every time she and Clayt had a little argument. It was the talk of the town, just the way she liked it."

Melody covered her face with her hands. She'd never gone in for gossip, and she used to completely tune it out whenever it had anything to do with Clayt and Victoria. Like a knife in her heart, hearing about them had been too painful.

Suddenly she remembered how Clayt had staggered backward when she'd told him she might want to go back to her apartment that day after they'd made love. Could he really believe *she* was anything like his tall, gorgeous, selfish first wife?

For a moment she wanted to give in to defeat and lay her head on her arms and close her eyes. *He thinks I'm like Victoria.* How could he?

She jumped to her feet, surprising herself as much as the other three women at the table. Jutting out one hip, she said, "Where does that man get off thinking I'm anything like that...that woman? I moved into his house and I'm helping him raise his daughter. I can't eat, I cry at the drop of a hat. It's all I can do to keep from curling up in a quiet corner and taking a nap in the middle of the day, yet I can't sleep at night. My body's so completely out of whack I swear my bras don't even fit the way they used to."

Melody stopped short. The awning over the front window flapped in the wind outside. Otherwise, the room was silent. Lisa, Jillian and DoraLee were all staring at her as if she'd grown a second nose. "What?" she asked.

"You and Clayt have been married almost three months haven't you?" Jillian asked quietly.

Nodding, Melody frowned in consternation.

"Your stomach's a little queasy and your emotions are a little out of kilter?" Lisa asked.

Melody nodded a second time. "You're both newlyweds. Do you think this is normal?"

Lisa and Jillian shared a meaningful look.

"It's normal," Lisa said, "if…"

"If what?" Melody asked.

"Have you been to see Doc Masey yet, sugar?"

"Doc Masey?"

Melody glanced around the table, her mind doing some fast mental math. "Do you think…?"

"It's possible, sugar."

Melody swallowed hard, struggling with her uncertainties. Recovering a little of her equilibrium with every breath she took, she said, "Oh, my."

Her thoughts were coming fast and furious. She'd been about to give up all hope of ever knowing Clayt's love, but if what her friends were insinuating was true, she had more reason than ever to keep trying.

"Lisa, have you gotten a new shipment of clothes in lately?" she asked thoughtfully.

Lisa McCully's brown eyes flashed. "Maternity clothes you mean?"

"No, at least not yet. Clayt's worried that I'll become like Victoria. I think it's time I opened my husband's eyes once and for all, don't you?"

"Who ever said nothing ever happens in small towns?" Jillian asked, an enchanting expression spreading across her face.

"What are you going to do?" Lisa asked.

"I don't have the details worked out yet, but I'm going to need a new outfit."

"Something red?" Lisa asked.

"Something flashy?" Jillian wondered aloud.

"I've got a better idea," Melody said, a knowing smile lighting her face. "But I might need a little help from my friends."

"Just name it," Lisa declared.

"Something tells me that brother-in-law of mine isn't going to know what hit him," Jillian exclaimed.

Melody smiled at her friends, her mind racing. Clayt wanted a wife who was nothing like Victoria? Whoever said to be careful what you wished for must have had Clayt Carson in mind.

Clayt pulled into his driveway and parked behind Mel's car. Rounding the front of his truck, he didn't know whether to whistle or grin. In the end, his mouth made the decision for him—a slightly out of tune rendition of "Let It Snow."

He'd gotten a call from the principal at Haley's school three days ago. It seemed his daughter had participated in a little incident involving a whoopee cushion and the seat of her teacher's chair. Clayt had agreed that Haley should write a paragraph about proper behavior and had taken away her television privileges for a week. Secretly he wasn't too upset. She was doing much better, but he could hardly expect a leopard to change its spots completely.

Haley was spending the night with his parents, who had arrived home yesterday, just in time for the Christmas holidays. That meant he and Mel had the evening to themselves. Yes sirree, things were definitely going well.

He'd been a little worried about Mel for a while there. She'd been quiet, lethargic, almost. But she'd been much more animated these past few days. At this rate she would be back to her old self in no time.

He hung his hat by the door and glanced around. Other than General Custer, who always met him at the door these days, the kitchen was empty. There was nothing bubbling on the stove. The television was tuned to a talk show in the next room, but Mel wasn't there, either. He found her in their bedroom. Although her back was to him, she appeared to be placing clothing in a bag.

He leaned in the doorway, enjoying the view, that old familiar heat stirring in his veins. Life was definitely good and getting better all the time. "Are you going somewhere, Mel?"

She jumped, turning so fast her hair swished against her cheek, one hand flying to her throat. "Clayt, I didn't hear you come in."

Ambling closer, he said, "It isn't often that we have the house to ourselves this time of day."

He intended to smooth her hair away from her face, but she spun away so fast his hand came into contact with only thin air. Undeterred, he followed her around the other side of the bed where he reached for her again. When she spun away a second time, his smile lowered a notch at a time. "Mel, what's going on?"

"Nothing," she said a little too quickly. "I'm due back at the diner in a few minutes, that's all."

"I thought Louetta was handling the supper crowd these days."

"She does. Usually."

Was it his imagination, or was Mel having a hard time meeting his eyes? She closed a drawer, grabbed the plastic bag lying on the bed and headed for the door. Shrugging into her coat, she turned around. "We'll still have the house to ourselves later, Clayt. In the meantime, why don't you come into the diner for supper?"

"What time?" he asked, his eyes getting stuck on the fullness of her bottom lip.

"Whenever you want. Just promise me you'll come." Again she didn't quite meet his eyes.

"Mel, what…"

She was gone before he could finish, and he was left trying to figure out what she was up to. Because she was up to something. He knew it just as surely as he knew it was going to snow.

Chapter Ten

Clayt waited until almost seven to head into Jasper Gulch for supper. He'd been right about the snow. Fat, wet flakes plopped down from the sky, gathering on fences and covering the brown landscape. The first parking space he could find was in front of the Clip & Curl. Other than a few pickup trucks lined up in front of the Crazy Horse Saloon, Main Street was usually deserted this time of night. What the hell was going on?

A blast of hot air hit him square in the face the instant he opened the diner's door. The place was packed, the noise level bordering on a low roar. Spotting Mel's one and only waitress serving apple pie to the Anderson brothers, who were making eyes at Brittany Matthews a few tables away, Clayt called, "Louetta, where's Mel?"

He didn't understand the reason behind Neil Anderson's hearty guffaw, but the blush on Louetta Graham's face was a sight for sore eyes. Fifteen years ago she'd been voted "the girl most likely not to" by her graduating class. Her blush was the only normal thing about the diner tonight.

"Clayt," Ned Anderson declared, "you're a lucky man."

"A lucky dog, you mean," Norbert declared, grinning like an idiot.

Glancing at cowboys and ranchers he'd known all his life, Clayt's trepidation grew by the second. All ten tables and four of the eight booths were occupied, most of them by men. He didn't like the looks of this one bit. Spying Luke and Wyatt at a nearby table, he headed in their direction. Cletus McCully grinned at him on the way by. Boomer Brown pushed at the brim of his hat and did the same. Clayt returned their greetings, but he couldn't shake the feeling that he was the only person in the room who wasn't in on the joke.

He'd almost reached Wyatt and Luke's table when he noticed a movement out of the corner of his eye. He took another step, then stopped cold.

He felt several pairs of eyes on him, but he couldn't take his eyes off Mel. She was wearing a short pink skirt and a gauzy white shirt that bared her shoulders. Her hair was fastened on top of her head with a ruby red clasp that matched the color of her lips. She looked like a neon sign. For what, he could only shudder.

And fume.

He'd taken a half-dozen steps by the time she'd refilled the O'Gradys' cups. If Rory O'Grady didn't stop staring at her chest, Clayt wasn't going to count how many steps it took to reach him and wring his womanizing neck.

"Easy, Clayt," Wyatt said, blocking his path and his view.

"Sit with us," Luke said.

"As soon as I flatten Rory's nose."

"There's no need to do that," Wyatt said quietly, his brown eyes watchful in case Clayt made a run for it. "You don't have to worry about that sister of mine. She can handle Rory O'Grady. If he gets too far out of line she'll thump him on the head with one of her trays and you know it.''

Clayt allowed Luke and Wyatt to lead him to their table, but he made certain his back was to the wall so he could see the entire dining room. The kitchen door swished open several times as Mel bustled in and out. Every man in the room reacted every time she came near. Animals one and all.

Clayt scowled, but he managed to keep his voice low and controlled as he turned to Wyatt and said, ''Are you going to arrest her or aren't you?''

Wyatt's grin was far from innocent. ''Arrest her for what?''

''For wearing a skirt that doesn't meet the limits of the law, dammit.''

Luke and Wyatt laughed. Clayt settled back into his chair, biding his time and biting his tongue.

''Clayt,'' Luke said, ''if you don't stop clenching your jaw you're gonna break a tooth.''

Clayt narrowed his eyes at his only brother. ''How would you like it if half the bachelors in the county were ogling your wife?''

''You think they haven't?'' Luke declared.

''Ninety percent of the men who go into Lisa's clothing store leave without buying anything,'' Wyatt said. ''You know the Jasper Gents, Clayt. They're just good old boys goin' along and gettin' along. And you can't really blame them for enjoying the view, now, can you?''

Clayt could blame them if he wanted to blame them, dammit.

The diner normally closed at seven. It was seven fifteen and not one of those good old boys Wyatt had mentioned appeared to be in any hurry to leave. Mel was the one who'd invited him to the diner for supper. Sooner or later she was going to have to mosey over to his table to take his order. When she did, he was going to get to the bottom of whatever the hell was going on.

It required every ounce of restraint Melody possessed to keep her lips from trembling as she made her way to Clayt's table. Even with the heat turned up, she felt a draft. It might have had something to do with the way she was dressed, but if this worked it would be worth a little discomfort. Besides, she hadn't been able to think of any other way. It was time to bring out the big guns. Subtlety wasn't working. She shouldn't have been surprised. When had Clayt Carson ever responded to anything subtle?

She hadn't thought she was the bold type, but drastic situations called for drastic measures. Wearing a short, skimpy skirt in November was about as drastic as she could get.

Now that she knew how humiliated Clayt had been when Victoria had run back to her apartment during their brief marriage, Melody understood his reasons for wanting her to lease her place over the diner. He didn't want history to repeat itself. Steadily making her way to his table, she had every intention of making a little history of her own.

She hadn't expected to do this in front of an audience, but gossip traveled faster than the speed of light in Jasper Gulch. The local boys who had stopped in for an early supper must have hightailed it back to the Crazy Horse and spread the word. Since she couldn't very well tell paying customers to leave, she did her best to ignore them. It wasn't difficult. Clayt drew her attention the way a moth was drawn to a flame.

"Hi, sweet pea," she murmured, stopping next to his chair. "I'm glad you could make it. Would you like your usual Thursday night special?"

"Sweet pea?" he sputtered.

Biting her lip to keep it from trembling, she said, "If

you're not ready to order, I could start you off with a cup of coffee.''

"Mel, what the hell are you doing?''

Fighting the urge to sink onto Clayt's lap and rest her aching feet, she cupped his lean cheek in one hand and said, "Why, I'm taking your order, of course.''

"I'm not hungry.''

"Just coffee, it is. I'll be right back with a cup.''

"Mel, wait.''

Clayt could still feel the imprint of her hand on his cheek, and if he lived to be a hundred, he'd never forget the way she turned around, as fair and graceful as a willow switch. "My name is Melody, remember?''

"All right, dammit, I'll call you Melody on one condition.''

She raised one penciled eyebrow and crossed her arms beneath her chest. The action drew the gauzy fabric of her blouse tight to her body. He could see the lacy edge of her bra through her blouse. It didn't take much imagination to picture what was beneath the next layer.

"What condition?'' she asked.

He shrugged out of his coat and placed it on her shoulders. "That you'll wear this.''

He heard a bell jingle and felt a draft as the diner's front door opened, but he didn't take his eyes off Mel...ody.

"All right, Clayt,'' she said, suddenly looking shy. "But before you say another word, there's something I want to tell you. You see, there's a reason for everything I've done tonight. I went to see...''

"Hello, darling. I'm back.''

A hush fell over the diner, but before Clayt could move, he heard the rustle of silk and cashmere and something blurred before his eyes. The next thing he knew he was being kissed soundly on the mouth.

Victoria.

Melody staggered backward. If it hadn't been for Wyatt's fast jump to his feet, she might have fallen right off her platform shoes. She appreciated the comfort of her brother's arm around her shoulders, but there wasn't much anybody could do about the ache in her throat or the tears that sprang to her eyes.

She'd forgotten how tall and beautiful and sophisticated Victoria was. The other woman's hair was a rich shade of brown and had probably been styled in one of the most expensive salons in the country. Surely her coat had cost more than Melody made in tips in a month. Her skin looked flawless, her lips set in a perfect pout as she said, "Darling, it's been so long."

Clayt hadn't seen or heard from Victoria since the day she'd dropped Haley on his doorstep in early spring. Wiping his mouth on the back of his hand, he scowled. That woman had always had lousy timing.

"Victoria," he gritted out. "What the hell are you doing here?"

"I wanted to surprise you. I've missed you, darling."

He might have bought her saccharine smile and innocent act once, but not tonight. "What about Haley?"

"Of course I've missed Haley. I have Christmas gifts for her in my car." She glanced over her shoulder at Melody. Batting fake eyelashes, she said, "I know it's probably too much to expect this hole-in-the-wall diner to have fresh lemons in December, but maybe you could ask little Daisy Duke here to bring us tall glasses of iced tea."

While everyone in the room gasped, Clayt was pretty sure he heard Cletus and Wyatt utter the same four-letter word. Narrowing his eyes at Victoria, he geared up to give her a piece of his mind. The soft flutter of Mel's fingertips grazing his arm kept him silent. Shrugging out of Clayt's jacket, she said, "Have a seat, Victoria. I'll bring your order right out."

Luke and Wyatt vacated the table. Victoria sank demurely into a nearby chair.

Melody strode into the kitchen in a daze. Moments later Louetta joined her in the quiet room. "You're not going to serve her iced tea, are you?"

Gripping the edge of the counter, Melody tried to decide what to do. Everything had gone so well. Now, it all seemed lost.

"Melody?" Louetta called softly.

Melody came out of her daze in slow motion. Feeling her wits rejuvenate, she poured two glasses of sparkling brown liquid over ice. Out of spite, she added a *fresh* slice of lemon to each.

"What are you going to do?" Louetta asked.

Taking both glasses, Melody turned toward the dining room. "Actually, I'm going to give that woman exactly what she deserves."

Plastering a smile on her face, she marched into the adjoining room. Peering down at Victoria, she said, "I might have been able to live with the way you looked down your nose at me. And I probably could have tolerated that disparaging comment about my diner. But when you kissed my husband on the mouth, you went too far. Maybe this will cool you off."

Raising the glasses to shoulder level, Melody moved them until they hovered directly over Victoria's lap.

"Clayton, do something!" Victoria gasped.

Haley used to call Clayt Clayton, too. Melody's hands shook, but she couldn't bring herself to dump the contents in Victoria's snooty little lap. No matter how Victoria looked down her nose at Melody, she was still Haley's mother. Haley loved her—God only knew why—and Melody couldn't bring herself to hurt somebody Haley loved.

"Clayton!"

Clayt heard Victoria's startled, though a trifle fake, cry,

but he couldn't take his eyes off Mel. How in the world could he have believed she was even remotely like Victoria? Victoria was beautiful in a hard, made-up sort of way. But Melody was beautiful in every way. Even in that gaudy getup. Melody's beauty came from the inside, where it danced and flickered like the glow of a candle in a soft summer breeze.

Clayt rose to his feet and reached for Melody's hand as if he'd done it a thousand times before. She made a startled sound in the back of her throat. Her eyes fluttered closed and her startled cry turned into a sigh the instant his mouth covered hers.

The kiss ended much more slowly than it had begun. Mel's eyes opened, her lips parted and finally lifted. It was all Clayt could do to keep from kissing her all over again. This close he could see the shadow of emotion in her eyes. An answering emotion beat in his own chest.

"Why, Clayton," Victoria taunted, "it looks as if you've lowered your standards."

Clayt glanced from one woman to the other. Now that he'd seen them side by side he couldn't believe it had taken him this long to recognize the difference between real beauty and trappings.

The diner was so quiet Clayt could have heard a pin drop. "Haley's spending the night with my parents, Victoria. I know she'll be happy to see you, and I'll arrange that this time. But she needs stability. Next time you're going to have to call first."

Victoria narrowed her eyes. After a long time, she glanced at the table where Melody had placed a glass of iced tea. Clayt's throat tightened as he waited to see what Victoria would do. Planting a perfectly manicured hand on her hip, she said, "I see."

Clayt doubted that. "She's happy, Victoria."

Victoria shook her head and pursed her lips. "I don't know how anybody could be happy in this town."

Clayt shrugged. He didn't think Victoria would be happy no matter where she was.

Ignoring all the folks who were watching her openly, she said, "I love Haley, no matter what anybody thinks, but I can't stay. I only stopped in to bring her Christmas gifts. I'll leave them at the ranch. Tell her I'll call her soon."

Always one for dramatic exits, she swished her hair behind her shoulders and twirled toward the door.

The Jasper Gents clapped the instant she was gone. Boomer whistled and Ned Anderson said, "I woulda dumped that iced tea in Victoria's snobby little lap."

"Yeah," Neil called. "Why didn't ya?"

Clayt snagged Melody's hand, drawing her gaze. "Because," he answered for her, "Melody's too big a woman for that."

The Jasper Gents mumbled their agreement. Still holding Melody's gaze, Clayt said, "Show's over everybody. The diner's closing for the night." With the lift of one eyebrow, he asked, "That all right with you?"

She nodded, and darned if she didn't grin. He had a sudden burning desire to sweep her into his arms and carry her to someplace quiet, someplace private. He glanced around the room. Wyatt and Luke had removed their hats and were grinning from ear to ear. Cletus snapped both suspenders and nodded for all he was worth. Jason Tucker looked about as pleased as Clayt had ever seen him. Even Rory O'Grady appeared happy with the way things had turned out. Louetta caught his attention from the other side of the room. With a blush tingeing her cheeks, she raised her voice and said, "Go ahead, you two. I'll close up."

Melody turned all at once and led the way to the kitchen. When she faced him behind the closed door, he saw in her eyes what he'd seen a little while ago. There was nothing more intoxicating than being wanted, accepted by this woman. And there was nothing more humbling than the fact that this chance at happiness had been right here all along.

"Melody, I've been such a fool."

"Don't you worry about it, Clayt," she whispered.

"You're forgiving me that quickly?"

She looked up at him the way she had a thousand times in the past. "Who said anything about quickly? I intend to give you the rest of your life to make it up to me."

He started to speak, but had to clear his throat and try again. Just when he thought he had Mel, make that Melody, all figured out, she went and said something that went straight to his head. His throat constricted and his heart beat a new rhythm. He was in for it with this woman. He'd known it the first time she'd kicked him in the shins when they were kids. Stepping back, he gave her a thorough once-over. She was trouble all right. It just so happened she was exactly the kind of trouble he wanted to get into.

Reaching for her hand, he drew her closer. "Has anyone ever told you that you have beautiful eyes? And a mouth that's perfect for kissing? I love you, *Melody*."

Melody's answer was lost in his kiss. Winding her arms around Clayt's neck, every thought but one was lost in his embrace. She loved this man with the rare smiles and strong hands, whose sense of honor was as steadfast as his passion. "Well, it's about time," she sputtered when their need to kiss gave way to their need to breathe. "I've been waiting all my life to hear you say that out loud, Clayt Carson." Raising her eyes to his, she whispered, "Say it again?"

"I'll say it again, a hundred times a day if you want. Or a hundred times a night." His eyes took on that sleepy glint that didn't necessarily mean he was sleepy, and his lips lifted in a devil-may-care smile.

"Clayt," she whispered, turning her head a heartbeat

before his lips could find hers a second time. "There's something I have to tell you."

He swung her into his arms so fast she gasped.

"Later," he growled. "Right now I have to get us to the nearest bed."

He didn't put her down until he'd kicked the door closed in her apartment. And then he only let her go long enough to wrap his arms around her and draw her close all over again. "Know what I'm going to do Melody?"

Her eyes got caught on his mouth. Although she was pretty sure she knew, she shook her head because she wanted to hear what he had in store.

Back-walking her toward her old bedroom, he said, "I'm going to kiss you. And then I'm going to kiss you some more."

Glancing at her dresser where the little kit she'd picked up at the drugstore in Murdo earlier in the week still sat in plain view, she said, "Clayt, this will only take a second."

"Believe me, it's going to take a lot longer than that. First I'm going to unbutton every one of those buttons of yours, one at a time. And when they're all open, I'm going to peel that shirt off you. And then your bra…"

"Clayt, really, there's something we have to talk about."

"I am talking…about what I'm going to do. Because I want to take a long look at you with nothing on, and when I can't stand just looking, I'm going to…"

He opened the top button with amazing ease. And then the second. And the third. "Clayt," she gasped when her shirt was sailing through the air behind her.

"I'm not going to stop until you want me to stop, not even if it takes until Tuesday."

Melody was drowning in sensation. Clayt loved her, and he wanted her, his hard body straining with need. "Hmm, Tuesday. I have a doctor's appointment on Tuesday."

"A doctor's appointment? Are you sick?"

She closed her eyes, a groan escaping her lips as her bra fluttered to the floor. "Sick?" she asked, her head lolling back. "Oh, no, I'm not sick, Clayt. I'm pregnant."

Clayt went perfectly still. "You're pregnant?"

She nodded.

"You're sure?"

"Pretty sure."

A smile spread across his face. "Hot dang. You always have managed to stay one step ahead of me."

"Then you're happy?"

He tossed his Stetson onto the dresser and yanked his shirt out of his jeans. His boots thudded to the floor. And then he was lowering her to the bed, kissing her all the while. "I love you, Melody. And yes, I'm happy. Something tells me I'm going to be even happier in a few minutes."

Melody might have boxed him in the arm, but she was too busy drowning in sensation at his touch, and at the way he was so intent upon removing her bright pink skirt. His fingers got tangled up in folds of satin. Clutching a handful of white fabric, he said, "What's this?"

Lovingly she smoothed her hand down the dress she'd laid across the bed the night she'd moved her things to the ranch. "It was my mother's wedding gown," she whispered. "I left it here, along with my dream of ever wearing it."

Something inside Clayt went very still. It wasn't his heart. That was beating like a freight train. It certainly wasn't his desire. That had never been stronger. It was the memory of a little girl with skinned knees and a long blond braid holding her brother's hand in a quiet country cemetery one long-ago spring day. That little girl had grown into an amazing woman. And she deserved to have her dreams come true.

Holding her face in both his hands, he swallowed the

lump in his throat and shuddered at the depth of emotion he felt at that moment. "Marry me again, in your mother's gown, in front of God and everyone. What do you say?"

Tears filled Melody's eyes at the depth of feeling in Clayt's voice. "All right," she whispered. "But, Clayt? Do you think you could finish making love to me first?"

She expected him to laugh. Instead, he kissed her cheek, her chin, her forehead. The moment before his lips found hers, she heard him whisper, "I'll see what I can do. And Melody? I'm beginning to think it was a good idea to keep your apartment."

Melody planned to tell him that Louetta had already signed a lease for the apartment and would be moving in the following week, but Clayt's hand glided over her waist and down her hip. Before long her eyes drifted closed and her breathing deepened and she sighed. Giving herself up to sensation, she decided to tell him later. Much, much later.

*   *   *   *   *

*Look for more romance from the folks in
Jasper Gulch, when Sandra Steffen's*
BACHELOR GULCH *miniseries continues.*
*Watch for NICK'S LONG-AWAITED HONEYMOON,
available in April 1998.*

Share in the joy of yuletide romance with brand-new
stories by two of the genre's most beloved writers

DIANA PALMER

and

JOAN JOHNSTON

in

LONE STAR CHRISTMAS

Diana Palmer and Joan Johnston share their favorite
Christmas anecdotes and personal stories in this
special hardbound edition.

Diana Palmer delivers an irresistible spin-off of her
LONG, TALL TEXANS series and Joan Johnston crafts an
unforgettable new chapter to **HAWK'S WAY** in this wonderful
keepsake edition celebrating the holiday season. So
perfect for gift giving, you'll want one for yourself...and
one to give to a special friend!

Available in November at your favorite retail outlet!

Only from

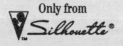

Take 4 bestselling love stories FREE

Plus get a FREE surprise gift!

Special Limited-time Offer

Mail to Silhouette Reader Service™

3010 Walden Avenue
P.O. Box 1867
Buffalo, N.Y. 14240-1867

YES! Please send me 4 free Silhouette Romance™ novels and my free surprise gift. Then send me 6 brand-new novels every month, which I will receive months before they appear in bookstores. Bill me at the low price of $2.67 each plus 25¢ delivery and applicable sales tax, if any.* That's the complete price and a savings of over 10% off the cover prices—quite a bargain! I understand that accepting the books and gift places me under no obligation ever to buy any books. I can always return a shipment and cancel at any time. Even if I never buy another book from Silhouette, the 4 free books and the surprise gift are mine to keep forever.

215 BPA A3UT

Name	(PLEASE PRINT)

Address	Apt. No.

City	State	Zip

This offer is limited to one order per household and not valid to present Silhouette Romance™ subscribers. *Terms and prices are subject to change without notice. Sales tax applicable in N.Y.

USROM-696

©1990 Harlequin Enterprises Limited

Daniel MacGregor is at it again...

New York Times bestselling author

NORA ROBERTS

introduces us to a new generation of MacGregors
as the lovable patriarch of the illustrious MacGregor
clan plays matchmaker again, this time to his three
gorgeous granddaughters in

THE MACGREGOR BRIDES

From Silhouette Books

Don't miss this brand-new continuation of Nora Roberts's
enormously popular *MacGregor* miniseries.

Available November 1997 at your favorite retail outlet.

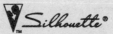 Silhouette®

As seen on TV!
Free Gift Offer

With a Free Gift proof-of-purchase from any Silhouette® book,
you can receive a beautiful cubic zirconia pendant.

This gorgeous marquise-shaped stone is a genuine cubic
zirconia—accented by an 18" gold tone necklace.

(Approximate retail value $19.95)

Send for yours today...
compliments of ▼ *Silhouette*®
™

To receive your free gift, a cubic zirconia pendant, send us one original proof-of-
purchase, photocopies not accepted, from the back of any Silhouette Romance™,
Silhouette Desire®, Silhouette Special Edition®, Silhouette Intimate Moments®
or Silhouette Yours Truly™ title available at your favorite retail outlet, together with
the Free Gift Certificate, plus a check or money order for $1.65 U.S./$2.15 CAN. (do
not send cash) to cover postage and handling, payable to Silhouette Free Gift Offer.
We will send you the specified gift. Allow 6 to 8 weeks for delivery. Offer good until
December 31, 1997, or while quantities last. Offer valid in the U.S. and Canada only.

Free Gift Certificate

Name: _____

Address: _____

City: _____ State/Province: _____ Zip/Postal Code: _____

Mail this certificate, one proof-of-purchase and a check or money order for postage
and handling to: SILHOUETTE FREE GIFT OFFER 1997. In the U.S.: 3010 Walden
Avenue, P.O. Box 9077, Buffalo NY 14269-9077. In Canada: P.O. Box 613, Fort Erie,
Ontario L2Z 5X3.

FREE GIFT OFFER   084-KFD
ONE PROOF-OF-PURCHASE
To collect your fabulous FREE GIFT, a cubic zirconia pendant, you must include this
original proof-of-purchase for each gift with the properly completed Free Gift Certificate.

084-KFDR

SILHOUETTE WOMEN KNOW ROMANCE WHEN THEY SEE IT.

And they'll see it on **ROMANCE CLASSICS**, the new 24-hour TV channel devoted to romantic movies and original programs like the special **Romantically Speaking—Harlequin™ Goes Prime Time**.

Romantically Speaking—Harlequin™ Goes Prime Time introduces you to many of your favorite romance authors in a program developed exclusively for Harlequin® and Silhouette® readers.

Watch for **Romantically Speaking—Harlequin™ Goes Prime Time** beginning in the summer of 1997.

If you're not receiving ROMANCE CLASSICS,
call your local cable operator or satellite provider and
ask for it today!

Escape to the network of your dreams.

See Ingrid Bergman and Gregory Peck in *Spellbound* on Romance Classics.

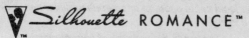

**Beginning in September
from Silhouette Romance...**

a new miniseries by
Carolyn Zane

They're a passel of long, tall, swaggering cowboys who
need tamin'...and the love of a good woman. So y'all
come visit the brood over at the Brubaker ranch and
discover how these rough and rugged brothers got
themselves hog-tied and hitched to the marriage wagon.

The fun begins with
MISS PRIM'S UNTAMABLE COWBOY (9/97)

"No little Miss Prim is gonna tame me! I'm not about to
settle down!"
—Bru "nobody calls me Conway" Brubaker
"Wanna bet?"
—Penelope Wainwright, a.k.a. Miss Prim

The romance continues in
HIS BROTHER'S INTENDED BRIDE (12/97)

"Never met a woman I couldn't have...then I met my
brother's bride-to-be!"
—Buck Brubaker, bachelor with a problem
"Wait till he finds out the wedding was never really on...."
—the not-quite-so-engaged Holly Fergusson

**And look for Mac's story coming in early '98 as
THE BRUBAKER BRIDES series continues, only from**

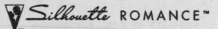

He's able to change a diaper in three seconds flat.
And melt an unsuspecting heart even quicker.
But changing his mind about marriage might take some doing!
He's more than a man...
He's a FABULOUS FATHER!

* * *

September 1997:
WANTED: ONE SON by Laurie Paige (#1246)
Deputy sheriff Nick Dorelli's heart ached for fatherless Doogie Clay—the
boy who should have been *his* son—and the woman who should have
been *his* wife. Could they all be blessed with a second chance?

November 1997:
WIFE WITHOUT A PAST by Elizabeth Harbison (#1258)
Drew Bennett had raised his child alone. But then the single dad discovered
his former bride Laura was *alive*—but didn't remember their wedded
estate! Could he make this wife without a past learn to love again?

January 1998:
THE BILLIONAIRE'S BABY CHASE by Valerie Parv (#1270)
Zoe loved little Genie as her own, so when the little girl's handsome
billionaire father appeared out of the blue to claim her, Zoe had only one
choice—to marry James Langford in a marriage of convenience.

* * *

Celebrate fatherhood—and love!—every month.
FABULOUS FATHERS...only in *Silhouette* ROMANCE™